SAVAGE
LUST

SAVAGE LUST

By Candi Scott

ASIN: B0DG6MCNCN

ISBN:

First Edition: September 2024

For Big Daddy, the OG, roaring down those streets of gold.

Warning: This novel is intended for readers 18+ and contains depictions of violence, drug use, and explicit sex.

CONTENTS

One

Riley

You don't belong here.

I circled the funeral home without stopping. A legion of terrifying Harley Davidsons filled the substantial parking lot, sometimes two or three to a space.

Mom had told me about the Desert Kings. These men were the stuff of nightmares, the boogeymen that hid in the shadows, and now my only lifeline. What would Mom think of me coming here?

She'd be furious.

But *she* hadn't left me any other options. I glanced at the large white envelope emblazoned with a courier's bright yellow logo that sat in my passenger seat. It mocked me with cheerily curved lettering.

I'd not fully investigated its contents, hadn't opened the sealed letters from my father. Sperm donor. Whatever you wanted to call him because he certainly *hadn't* been a part of my life. Which was amusing since Mom had thought she'd done so well to hide us.

A lawyer had sent cash and a written summons. The gist: *come to Nevada* and *there is more where that came from.*

All it would take was a trip to the desert. The money in the envelope might be enough to keep the debt collectors at bay if I didn't spend too much of it.

But nowhere near enough to give me a roof over my head, go back to college, and get the hell out of California.

Well, it *had* been enough for the last.

My father was a Desert King Motorcycle Club member that my mom said she barely escaped from. She blamed him for everything wrong in her life—and mine.

And still, showing up at his viewing unannounced seemed disrespectful. So would being at the funeral, but...

The lawyer will be there tomorrow and he says I have to go.

With the address the lawyer had given me keyed up on my GPS, I drove instead to my dad's home. Not like I could afford a hotel, anyway. I was clinging to what little cash I now had, like it was the last of it. As one did when you'd spent the better part of a year near to starving without a dime to your name.

It was a pretty house, painted a pale blue in defiance against the earth tones of his neighbors. The cool colors were a surprise from a man in his fifties, with no family, that ran an outlaw biker gang.

The clay tiled roof and an assortment of decorative succulents dotting the pebbled sidewalk were downright cozy.

There were worse places to spend a few days.

The keys jangled as I shook them from the envelope and made a note of the alarm code. I unlocked the door, silenced said alarm, and let myself in. I flicked on a lamp and wrestled with the feeling of wrongness, of being in someone's home unannounced.

Once my nerves settled, I ducked from room to room to ensure I was alone.

I'd wondered if he'd had a live-in girlfriend, or something...but the place was empty. Only one bedroom in use and only a man's jacket on the rack by the door.

The letter said he would leave most everything to me, including his house. I just needed to be present for the funeral and in a few weeks, for the reading of the will. In a twisted sort of way, this was mine. Who else would be here?

The place was tidy but masculine. The walls were light and the furniture dark. Political thriller paperbacks and motorcycle magazines littered the coffee table. Coffee cups displaying motorcycle logos hung on a rack by the coffeepot in the kitchen. A well-used set of socket wrenches lay open on the counter by the back door with several missing. I ran my fingers over them, as if they might somehow tell me who he was.

In the hallway, I flicked on a light to see a trail of framed images dotting the walls. Some of bikes, glossy and chrome, others of men with beards and leather vests, most smiling or joking. Even faded family photos of grandparents and others I'd never met. I recognized young Rick Bowman from some of Mom's old pictures she'd kept hidden in a drawer. That's how I'd always imagined my dad, young and vibrant, the romantic product of childhood nosiness.

I closed my eyes against the last memories of Mom, frail and dying, the exact opposite.

Several newer frames, those same men but older...but this, this would have been the man I'd known. Long hair, going gray, lean face with the same angular shape as mine. Crinkles at the corners of his eyes. Something inside me ached, wondering briefly if Mom had been wrong about him.

One of him with a teenager, a gangly boy that was more arms and legs, than anything else, caught my attention. The same young man was in several more. A warm sort of jealousy lit low in my belly for a kid I'd never met—but why?

Because he knew him and you didn't.

I shoved the unwanted emotion aside. This had never been about me. Whatever issues had been Rick's. Or Mom's. Or both.

I stalked toward the master bedroom and flicked on a light. There were other bedrooms, I'd seen them as I'd sneaked around to see if anyone was home. But something drew me here. I picked up a pillow and inhaled. The scent of spicy aftershave and mint triggered an unfamiliar ache of longing. At least when he'd been alive, I'd known he was out there somewhere. It had made losing Mom easier to stomach. I hadn't truly been alone, even if he was a stranger to me.

Now I was.

A floorboard creaked, and I tilted my head. The quiet was so consuming, that when I listened closely, my own breath drowned everything out.

I turned as a dark blur flashed in the doorway. I had enough time to squeal before I was knocked back and pinned to the mattress. I fought against the weight of my attacker, thrashing and wriggling frantically, twisting in the bedcovers, and knocking the pillows askew.

Underneath one was a pistol. I snaked one hand free and reached for it.

"Whoa, not so fast, sweetheart." The sharp, biting command from a masculine voice stopped me for the scantest second before he encircled my wrist again.

Survival instinct flared to life and I turned enough to knee him in the groin and leap for the gun.

As my attacker rolled to the floor, I jumped off the other side of the bed, clutching the gun between trembling hands. It was heavier, colder than I imagined. The way people swing pistols around in movies, you'd think they were much lighter.

He rose from the floor, still clutching his groin, red-faced and groaning. "The fuck?" he gasped out and glared at me.

I could finally make out his face. The clear blue of eyes beneath gold-tipped lashes, the shock of blond hair pushed back from his face—I recognized him. It was the kid from the pictures. Sure, he was older and filled out, with facial hair surrounding his mouth and covering his chin. Same guy, just older and significantly more handsome.

The alarm bells in my brain lessened, but I kept the pistol pointed at him.

Something in his face changed, a brief flash of recognition as the red seeped out of his cheeks. He rose to his full height and raised both hands in the air in front of him.

"Riley?" The voice wasn't as cold or harsh now. Deep, but clear and quiet.

Something about that tone slipped in, comforted me, and my body relaxed, the gun dipping. He knew me.

"How do you know my name?" The control I had over my voice was surprising. Only marginally shrill. "And what are you doing here?"

His grin was slow to spread across his lips. Like somewhere along the way he'd decided he shouldn't and then the devil on his shoulder convinced him otherwise. "Sweetheart, I'd feel a lot more like answering your questions if you'd point that elsewhere."

"I'd feel a lot better once I know who the fuck you are."

"I live here." He lowered his hands and seemed to shift closer to the corner of the bed. "I'm a friend."

"Now you're going to tell me my estranged biker father had a younger, live-in lover?"

He snorted. "What? Hell no. I live in the apartment above the garage."

"That doesn't explain what you..." I waved the gun in a small circle. "Were about to do to me."

He recoiled with an irritated flinch. "Fuck no. You're Archer's daughter." Then he gestured with a roll of his shoulder and a wink. "Ain't never had to force no one, sweetheart. Not even one as pretty as you."

None of that explained how he knew me, why he'd come in here...or any of it. I was shaken, tired, and quickly losing patience.

"That make you my long-lost brother, then?"

"Ha. No." He laughed outright, and it wasn't until he brushed a hand over his goatee, I realized he'd come completely around the bed.

Before I could jerk away, he'd wrenched the pistol from my hands by the barrel, spun it toward the wall and pulled the trigger.

I threw my hands over my ears, but instead of a deafening boom, there were only three quiet clicks.

"Chamber a round and flick the safety off before you threaten to shoot someone." With the sure confidence of long practice, he dropped the magazine and cleared the gun.

The place between shock and humiliation is weird. My skin flushed and the room sort of faded in and out. The only thing I could see was this cute guy glaring at me like I'd just walked in and screwed up his entire world.

He hadn't had a father who never lifted a hand to help show up dead out of nowhere. Neither had I...until now. This entire thing was a shit show.

I didn't know if I could trust him, but I was literally pinned between him and a wall and trying really hard not to laugh or cry or both.

Then he surprised me. "Want a beer?"

Without waiting for a response, he turned and stalked from the room. I got a good look at the back of his vest. Desert Kings MC. He was a member of Rick Bowman's motorcycle club. Not how I envisioned my introduction to these guys.

I followed him, not so much for the beer, but propelled by some sort of enigmatic force. If he was even a little like how Mom had described these guys, I should be running the other way. Instead, I was slinking into the kitchen, looking at my feet, thankful he couldn't read my mind.

If he could, he'd be getting up close and personal with how much I'd enjoyed having him on top of me. A scuffle on the bed had been better than my sweaty, awkward, high school make out session with the neighbor.

With a guy like this, things would be very different.

My cheeks heated with the thought.

"What are you doing here, darlin?"

"Riley." I sat at the scuffed, round wooden table and took the beer he handed me. "But you already knew that."

No way was he more than five years older than me, if that. In the kitchen light, his face was younger—like he wore the goatee to hide his age. Either way, the look was disarming. Everything about him was, especially when he grabbed a pint of ice-cream and a spoon and leaned against the counter while I nursed the beer.

When he caught me staring, he saluted me with the spoon. "I need a clear head." His eyes were bloodshot, his face still flushed. Weed, alcohol, whatever it was, I doubted he'd been crying in a funeral home pew. "Now, answer my question." But there was a cool, commanding way he said it. Like he expected people to tell him everything he wanted to know.

"This is my father's house." I clutched the beer between us. Not that it was a shield against anything. I didn't relax. The way he'd taken the gun from me and skillfully unloaded it was kind of scary—and exciting.

He'd already proved that I didn't stand a chance, physically, at defending myself. I should be scared, yet I wasn't. I was too tired to calculate the risk. The adrenaline was wearing off and left me deflated and tired.

The worst part was, I had nowhere else to go.

He pulled the spoon between his lips, licking it clean. My eyes hung to every motion, no matter how hard I tried to look away. "No shit. Same father you've never been to visit."

I took a long swallow, tried not to choke on the thickness of the beer—the almost bread like taste. Anything to distance myself from the seething accusation in his voice. "Not that it's any of your business, but he didn't seem to want much to do with me. The first contact I had with him was a letter from his lawyer that he died."

He paused with a spoon full of ice cream a few inches from his lips. "When was that?"

"Fuck off." I needed to be nicer. I had the feeling that if he didn't want me here, it would be a problem. I didn't need any more of those. I had plenty already.

I never imagined my life would come down to having to ass kiss some random biker douche just to survive.

Could be worse. I gripped the bottle tight and tried not to think about the shifty truckers and drug dealers that populated the truck stop I'd slept at for months.

He didn't respond but ate his ice cream like it was the last remaining tether to his patience and waited for me to cave. Because he knew I would. Guys like him were used to always getting their way.

"Earlier this week. I have to be here for the reading of the will *and* the funeral." My inner independent woman groaned.

"Give you keys?"

"Yes. And the code."

He acted so at ease, so at home here, and it grated on my nerves. "My turn. Who are you?"

"Cam." He finished off the container and tossed it into the bin a few feet away with a swish of the bag, then dropped the spoon into the empty sink with a clatter.

"Let me see your phone." He pushed off the counter, hand extended. I was handing it to him before I thought better of it.

His fingers flew across the screen before he passed it back. "If you need me, call me." He headed toward the door stopping to slip the gun into his pocket. "Set the alarm, get some rest. I'll be back in the morning before the funeral."

He didn't ask why I wasn't staying at a hotel and of that, I was grateful. One humiliating moment a night was my limit.

I watched the way her ass swayed, the short skirt teasing a view that never came. Yeah, I could fuck her six ways from Sunday.

But I didn't want to.

The other guys were seated around the large oak table when I walked in. Preacher at his new seat at the head. My gut clenched so hard I had to fight to keep one foot in front of the other as I took my seat. Much like Archer, the older man was tall. Unlike Archer, he was round in the middle and had to push back from the table to make room for the bulge of his gut.

Too much beer and not enough cardio.

"What's up, brother?" Preacher asked me, his salt and pepper eyebrows knitted with concern like mocking, angry steel wool.

"Change of plans for tomorrow." I leaned back in my seat, rubbed a tired hand across my face.

And if I'd ever thought I couldn't shock the table, I'd been damn wrong.

"The funeral is covered," Drop Top Randy grumbled, annoyed that he'd had to be the go between with the funeral home director. The squat man was as tall as he was round, his dumpy stature being what earned him his nickname. His oddly impeccable organizational skills were how he kept his secretary role term after term.

"Archer's kid is here." Ignoring the rest of the table, I watched Preacher's expression turn from worn out leather to granite, as he hid his reaction.

Yeah, you weren't prepared for this.

"Archer had a kid? How old is he?" Jester asked, voice clear despite the shock on his face. One of the younger crew, one of my boys, it wasn't a surprise Jester didn't know.

"She." AP responded before I could. "Probably about twenty."

AP Merrick was Archer's best friend since birth, a founding member of the club. And one of the two men at the table I fully trusted. No surprise he'd known about Riley. He'd been around when she was born.

Recovering, Preacher zeroed in on me. "How'd you know she was here? She call you? Already bagging her, son?" He snorted a half laugh, but his gaze held a glint of meanness.

"She was at the house when I got back."

A few curse words, some surprised faces. Nothing I hadn't expected or needed to see. I held Preacher's gaze. Once, I'd watched a documentary about prey animals and how they frantically glance around for places to run when a predator watched them. *Nah, Preach, I'm a fucking lion.* I leaned back in my seat, grinned a little.

"Said the lawyer contacted her. She'll be here for the funeral tomorrow."

"That's why you called this meeting?" Preacher's eyes narrowed. He thought I was just a young idiot that Archer gave too much power.

Fuck him.

"With next of kin, there are changes to make for tomorrow." Drop Top groaned. "I fucking hate this position. None of you degenerates die on my watch. I ain't fucking doing it again. But I'll wake up the goddamn mortician and get this set up."

"Thanks, brother." I stopped shy of sighing.

The short, dumpy man with the ruddy complexion reached across the table to bump his fist against mine.

"You running interference with the daughter?" Preacher asked me, his voice unusually amicable. "Or you want me to? I know it's been rough for you this week."

I'd kill him before he got anywhere near her. His gambling habit wasn't the only thing that had almost cost him his cut. "I got it. She knows me, and I'm already there." The protective rush for someone I'd just met pitched my stomach.

That surge of emotion was something I'd have to throttle back. It had been a long time since I felt anything—I blocked everything out. Losing Archer had stirred up a variety of dangerous thoughts. I wasn't anyone's savior. I was my own man.

I'd keep Riley safe, and then get her the fuck out of Dry Valley. Once she was gone, one less thing for me to worry about. Because I didn't need a woman making shit harder for me.

"Car will be there for her in the morning." Drop Top grumbled, making notes on his phone.

"One more thing," Preacher interjected, rolling the gavel around in his hand. "I'm going to give the Ukrainians another go, see if they'll come off some guns for Wanda's boys."

Wanda, Queen of the trailer park and Nevada's most prolific meth cook. I recoiled at the thought of her.

Merc cleared his throat before speaking. "Ky said no. I don't see that changing."

"He doesn't call the shots, the uncles do. I'm going to see them."

I'd known Merc most of my damn life, but there was some shit we didn't talk about. Whatever he had going on with the Ukrainian mob was one of them. He knew them, so we all deferred to him.

"It's not going to do any good." His voice even, his expression never changed. He thought Preacher's play was a stupid one. I could read it all over his non-reaction.

"I'll see about that." Preacher puffed up, clearly disbelieving. His ego couldn't bear to hear no.

"That it?" AP prodded Preacher before that topic could turn into an argument.

"Yeah." He grumbled low and smacked the gavel on the table to signify the meeting over, frowning as he processed.

That went smoother than I thought. I was halfway out the door before Preacher called to me. "We need to have a sit down, you and me. Soon."

"The fuck for?" I turned back. I'd adamantly opposed his goon Paul's seat at the table. There had been better options, more loyal guys with longer standing. And that was just one thing in a long list of shit Preacher wanted done I didn't agree with. "It is what it is."

Three

Riley

For the first time in weeks, I slept. But not until I was reassured by the low rumble of Cam's bike as he parked it out back. Something about being alone, but not alone, in the house, was soothing. No worrying about some rapist or robber breaking the window in my car and pulling a gun on me. The fear of resting in parking lots in my car—gone.

At least my father had given me that.

The sound of Cam's motorcycle, leaving before the funeral, woke me.

There was a text on my phone, sent before he left. A weird bubble of excitement caught in my throat, then quickly deflated when I read it.

Desert Kings are sending a car to pick you up. Be ready by 10:30.

What had I expected? I'd not even known the guy twenty-four hours. I stood and rubbed the sleep from my eyes. He probably left every woman he met excited and chasing after him. He had the fuck boy swagger down, better than any I'd ever seen.

Not that I'd met many.

I turned my focus to the things that mattered, not the sexy biker next door. What was I supposed to wear to the funeral of a man I'd never met?

My father's funeral.

I settled on a modest black dress that swayed around my knees. Nothing remarkable, something that should blend. Though, the only shoes I had to match were knee high black leather boots. My club shoes. I snorted at my reflection. Wearing these, I'd fit in even better.

The car that arrived was a black stretch limousine. The sort of thing celebrities were carted off to award shows in. I looked up one side of the street and down the other before a driver in a crisp white shirt climbed from the front seat.

"Riley Bowman?" He made his way to the back door.

I blinked at the pomp and circumstance. "Yeah." This was definitely over the top.

He swung an arm toward the door. "I'm Tommy. Sorry to hear about your dad."

What was I supposed to say to that? I knew Tommy as well as I had my father. Archer Bowman was a stranger. The more reminders of that I was hit with, the more I second guessed coming here at all. "Thank you."

I tucked myself into the limo and tried my best to settle in. Tommy had closed the partition between us. I was grateful, because small talk wasn't something I was good at. Alone, hidden from the outside world, it was easier to gather myself and prepare for what was coming.

They were all strangers. People he'd chosen over me. And here I was, fulfilling his warped last wishes for what—money?

That you desperately need.

I could hear Mom's voice now, warning me how dangerous he was—they were. To get out while I still had the chance. I trembled. Not because I was afraid, but because I should be and wasn't. Her illness had changed me, broken a part of me.

To keep from thinking about all the things I was missing, all the things I could have had—I stared out the dark tinted window at the Nevada desert. It had been full dark when I arrived in Dry Valley, so the brilliance of the sun shining off the hard packed earth and the red hills in the distance was unexpected. I could see why Archer chose to make his life here.

I fought back the tears that threatened. I hadn't lost just my future, but the only parent I'd ever known. She'd been as steady for me as any rock, and I missed her so much I ached. Since it was just the two of us, there'd been no funeral for her, just a pretty wooden box filled with her ashes.

A spitting, rumbling reverberation jerked me from my thoughts. Two rows of bikes passed us on each side. Each rider giving the limo—giving me—a two-finger salute as they passed.

An odd, warming emotion started in my chest and worked its way up the back of my throat. I wouldn't say I was soothed, but the show of respect hit me in a way I hadn't expected. I liked that it made me feel important.

I needed to meet with the lawyer and get the hell out of here. Cam was dangerous. Hadn't he proved it in the way he'd grabbed me, attacked me? It was practically assault and yet I spent all night remembering the brief contact of his hands on my body. Gooseflesh covered my skin and pleasure tingled between my thighs each time I brought up the memory, making it dirtier than it was.

I liked it.

Daughter of the outlaw biker shouldn't be such a shock. I wasn't a total prude.

The bikers flanked the limo all the way to the funeral chapel. What was it about Rick Bowman that made him so important? Why the big fanfare? All I'd known was that he'd been part of a biker gang—Motorcycle Club. But this amount of reverence was a lot. Especially for a notoriously violent drug dealer that Mom had been terrified of.

The knot in my stomach twisted around an anchor and held me molded to the seat. The limo pulled in behind the hearse under an awning. I didn't get out. My heart throbbed in my ears, and that weight in my stomach bobbed up and down in the acid that churned. It was too late now, I couldn't turn and run.

My door opened and a tall masculine form blocked out the bright desert sun. It wasn't until he bent into the car and extended his hand that I realized it was Cam.

"Come on, Riley." His grip was warm on mine as he helped out. Metal winked from his leather vest as he did.

All around me, Harleys were shutting off as those that rode with the limo pulled in behind us. Those already there, leather vests covered in patches, milled about and all stared openly at me. Cam caught my elbow and held me steady when I stumbled as trepidation seeped in.

"You okay?" There was a slight tenderness in his expression that hadn't been there the night before.

"They're all staring at me," I whispered.

"It's about to get worse." He snorted, but stopped at the hood of the car when he noticed my reluctance. He shifted, so that his body blocked me from their view, and leaned down so that it seemed as if he were consoling me.

"Most of them had no idea you existed until this morning. Archer..." He trailed off with a whispered curse and rubbed a hand over the blond hair that surrounded his mouth. "He didn't tell many people.

"There'll be some push back, but not today. They'll all show you more respect than anyone in the room."

For what? Coming here was a bad idea. I needed to leave. Mom was right, these were bad people. "What do I tell them?"

"Whatever the fuck you want, darlin."

I opened my mouth to tell him—what, exactly, that I didn't want anything? But a large, broad shouldered, potbellied man interrupted me. His handlebar mustache was flecked with so much gray I couldn't tell what color it had originally been. And his hair was coarse, likely looking unkept seconds after he'd tried to do anything with it.

Across the right side was a bright, new patch that read *President*. I flicked a glance to Cam's. *Vice President*.

That surprised me. Cam was so much younger than all the others.

"Hey there, Riley. I'm Greg Lowell, but everyone calls me Preacher." He sucked his tongue across his teeth like he was picking them.

The way he hovered and leered put everything into perspective. This was the sort of man who scared women, the sort that should scare me. Gathering myself took a lot more effort than it should have. But after several long seconds, I managed a facade of calm deference and shook his hand.

Then I scooted closer to Cam, fighting for an appropriate mix of fascination and sorrow. When all I wanted to do was run. I turned myself into what they needed to see. Pretty, decorative, and questionably devastated. The things expected of a young woman who had never met the man she was here to bury.

Cam took a few steps away, half hugging a man who approached. They were all dressed the same, one leather vest blurring into the next. Two rows of gleaming Harleys flanked the hearse, but there was one sitting out front all alone, sunlight glinting off the polished chrome. A group of them stood around it, as if somehow they were saying goodbye.

"You have our deepest condolences." Preacher pounced into the space between Cam and me, leaning in, brushing his handlebar mustache against my cheek as he kissed me. I jerked when he pressed a hand to the small of my back.

I flinched and caught Cam's eyes over Preacher's shoulder. His gaze was hard but searching. As if with one word, he'd barrel over there and jerk the other man off me. I blinked once and Preacher straightened and smiled down at me, asking something about the ride over. He wore too much cologne and it clung to me enough that I almost gagged.

Uncomfortable, I murmured what must have been a suitable answer, because with his hand still on my back he led me toward the chapel. I looked around as we went, trying to ignore the skin crawling sensation that traveled up from his touch.

Cam stood at the end of the row, lighting a cigarette as he studied the motorcycle in front of the hearse.

I didn't need anyone to tell me that the gleaming machine was my father's.

***

Inside, there were more people than I could have imagined. I'd never suffered from stage fright, but as Preacher guided me between the pews toward the front, my palms were sweaty, and my knees wobbled.

At the first long row draped in a gold tasseled banner that read *RESERVED*, a few people huddled together. Two were men dressed similarly to Cam and Preacher. The other, an attractive woman about my age.

"AP, this is Archer's daughter, Riley." Preacher spoke at a respectable volume, ensuring that anyone close heard him. Like he was parading me around as some sort of macabre trophy.

A man about Preacher's age, with shaggy dark hair that hung over his ears, extended his hand. The gentle smile that spread on his handsome face hinted at how good-looking he'd once been. "I'm sorry we're meeting this way, Riley. This is my son, Jace, and daughter Dylan."

He gestured to a younger man, quite obviously his son, who extended a long fingered, calloused hand. Yeah, AP was definitely smoking hot as a younger man—considering his son was practically a clone. Complete with the snug-fitting jeans and black leather vest.

But he was different. Jace Merrick looked like a man simultaneously comfortable in his own skin but uncomfortable in the room. He was constantly tense, ready for a fight and likely marking every avenue of escape.

A dark beard covered his face, as if he needed more than the shaggy hair to hide behind. And yet, he stood tall and unafraid. He'd just rather be anywhere else. A kindred spirit, it seemed. I shook Jace's hand as he sized me up in a different way than his father. But unlike Preacher's ogling, I almost wanted to preen as he gave a short, approving jerk of his chin.

I hadn't been found wanting.

Then he looked over my shoulder and smiled with the ease of long friendship.

I followed his gaze to see Cam right behind me. His blue eyes were dark like impending rain, his mouth twisted in a half-amused smirk.

My gaze shifted between the two of them as Jace snickered a little and ducked his head, hiding it with a cough. It's like they had a silent conversation and had done so countless times before. I was intrigued.

Preacher rubbed a small circle on my back and I stepped away as tendrils of cool apprehension skittered across me. I stood closer to Jace, right between he and Cam now and immediately felt safe.

"Hi, Riley." The young woman shouldered in between us with a dramatic elbow to Jace's side. She brought us all back to the moment.

Dylan Merrick put the capital Vs in *Va Va Voom*. She wore a pretty, maroon dress with white flowers that hugged more curves than a back road. The dark red lipstick seemed brighter against the chocolate hair that framed her face and bright blue eyes.

For the first time, the expression staring back at me was understanding. She put me at ease immediately. I relaxed even more when Preacher ambled off with AP. The air suddenly easier to breathe.

"It's customary for the family to wait near the coffin, let the guys come through and pay their respects." Dylan's husky voice was soft and coaxing. "A lot of them came from other states. Archer was the founding father of the club."

My eyes snapped toward the coffin, one end open, dozens of flower displays surrounding it. More than a few draped with Desert King banners. But none of that mattered, only the casket itself and the body memorialized inside it.

"I..." panicked, unable to form a real word I stuttered. I hadn't seen him in life. Walking up to the casket itself would make me a fraud.

A warm hand took mine, squeezing a little. The rough pad of a thumb brushed a soothing rhythm over my knuckles. "You don't have to look, but we would appreciate it if you would greet people for a little while before we start." Cam's voice was so buttery smooth that I wanted to brush against him and purr.

The back and forth of my emotions made me dizzy.

Then he brushed his lips across my ear so only I could hear. "Remember, they don't know you or anything about you. They have nothing to judge."

Gooseflesh rippled in the wake of his warm breath and I managed to nod once. Cam led me hand in hand to an area just past the coffin. I was a fraud, an imposter. The letter from the lawyer had said I was supposed to show up, not be paraded around like some sort of freak.

I could leave, go back sleeping in my car, pretend none of this happened, and nobody would stop me. But when I peered at Cam, he had glanced into the coffin. His chest hitched and pain seeped into his features. I might be a fraud, but he wasn't.

I stayed.

One person's face faded into the other until I was adrift in a sea of pitying glances and half-hearted hugs. Cam stayed close, though, and held court. He knew this was a ruse, a show, and he was the one directing it. Every person that approached was eating out of his hand before they walked away.

The easy confidence was sexy.

As Cam led me to the reserved row, the entire chapel stared at me with pity as they took their seats. Men in leather vests stood along every wall and in every corner. Panic bloomed in my chest and my skin grew hot. These were the boogeymen of my childhood. Every time she'd seen a man on a Harley, Mom had stopped to tell me how dangerous they were.

Cam squeezed my hand and pulled me toward the padded bench. As I sat, he draped his arm over my shoulder and the panic faded. How could he be that dangerous?

The service itself didn't take long. I sat between Cam and Dylan on a wooden pew in the first row, as if they were afraid to leave me alone. Maybe they were. The preacher talked, then AP gave the eulogy. Emotion threaded each story he told, painting a picture of a fun loving, larger-than-life character that cared for his biker family very much.

But abandoned his only child.

After a final prayer, six leather clad bikers picked up the casket and carried it outside. Dylan did her best to usher me past the remainder of offered condolences, but it still took us so long that when we made it through the crowd, the hearse and limo were ready. I stopped, watching as they closed the door on the flower draped casket. It seemed so formal for the jovial, partying man AP had spoken of.

Cam had mounted the large, gleaming Harley in the front. The throbbing of the engine reverberated through the awning.

"He's riding Archer's bike?" My question held no accusation.

Dylan gave a solemn nod of her head. "All the patch members give their burial wishes. Archer's was that if anyone rode his bike after he died...it be Cam."

I didn't know my dad, but I understood the pain I'd seen on Cam's face. I'd lost the only family I'd ever known, too. That was a kinship forged in a sort of pain that couldn't be described.

If I wanted to say a proper goodbye to the man he'd loved, the man who'd given me life, I couldn't do it tucked away behind tinted glass, alone.

Without a word to Dylan, I moved toward the group of bikers that had surrounded Cam. I didn't need to ask them to move; they parted for me without question. He killed the engine, his brow knitted with curiosity.

"Can I ride with you?" I looked outward, down the highway, unable to look at Cam or face the gazes that had all turned to me. "I figured it's a good way to say goodbye."

"Fuck." He cursed under his breath and stood, swinging his long leg over the bike. He popped the helmet off his head and shrugged out of his vest, handing both to AP, whose eyes were bloodshot from unshed tears.

"Glad you wore boots." The older man mumbled through his grief.

Cam unbuttoned the black and white flannel shirt he wore, then tossed it over my shoulders like a matador. "It'll be cooler than you think."

"And the bugs suck." Jace gave a somber grin.

Cam buttoned the shirt down my front with quick, precise motions of his long fingers, while I shoved my arms through the sleeves. When he took his vest back, AP pushed Cam's helmet onto my head and tightened the chin strap. It was heavy, but open faced and not as cumbersome as I'd imagined.

"What about him?" I gestured to Cam.

"He's hardheaded." AP patted my helmet.

Cam had already fired the bike back up but stayed standing astride it as I gathered my skirt between my thighs and threw my left leg over behind him.

"Put your feet on the pegs, don't burn your legs on the tail pipes."

I did as I was told, tucking my skirt between us. It would fly out some, but at this point I didn't care.

When he sat and kicked up the kickstand, other bikes fired up all around us. The throbbing cacophony grew so loud it swallowed up every other sound for miles. Cam reached back and pulled both my arms around his waist, so I was forced to press my body closer to him.

He caught my gaze in the rear-view mirror on the handlebars. *Hang on.*

And I did, Cam idling the bike to the entrance to the funeral home before letting it rip on his way out. The bike roared to life between my legs, and the earth suddenly zipped by so fast I couldn't do anything but cling to his waist.

Then I turned my face to the sun.

A normal person would be scared. I wasn't. This was exhilaration, this was a thrill that soared up from the vibration of the motorcycle all the way to the tips of my fingers that trembled against Cam's abdomen.

At a large curve, I held tighter to him, pressed my body against the warm leather that covered his strong back. The bite of the wind blistered at my cheeks but wasn't unpleasant. I could feel—everything. For the first time since Mom died, I felt alive.

On the back of that bike, I could *feel*.

Four

CAM

Riley pressed against me wasn't the distraction I needed. My body demanded a reaction, to lay a hand on her bare knee, rub back against her thigh, push that skirt up higher.

I sank my teeth into my bottom lip, using the pain to chase away the image of her creamy thighs, untouched by the sun, stretched across the back of the bike.

Jesus, you need some ass, Savage.

I could almost hear Archer's deep, scratchy voice, see him rolling his eyes and reminding me that chasing tail would get me in trouble. Would he care that it was his daughter I was fantasizing about? Probably not. He'd be pissed I was riding his bike.

Or maybe he would. I sure as hell wouldn't tell him. He had his reasons to keep her away. Guys like me were probably at the top of that list.

A different sort of pain clogged my throat. I didn't realize grief had stolen my breath until Riley squeezed tight around a turn and forced it out of my chest. This grief was heavier than when my mom died. Then I'd been angry at the world, too angry and scared to feel the pain.

This was the first time the loss ripped through me like a bullet, burning everything it touched until I couldn't breathe.

I hadn't cried, hadn't had a chance. Some of the other guys had at the funeral, even AP's hard as stone ass had spent days red eyed. Preacher hadn't cried. He'd barely reacted at all and he'd found the body.

Riley had held up pretty well. Considering Preacher had been all over her like grease on an axle.

The exhaust rumbled in protest when I flexed my fist around the throttle. The anger and suspicion chased away some of the pain. I clung to those feelings, clenching my jaw and getting on the engine a little more.

I made the turn off the highway and glanced in the mirror. Riley's eyes were closed, her angular, pretty face serene as she turned it toward the sun. The anger, the speculation, all faded away and a warmth spread across my chest and down to where it simmered beneath her touch.

She was fucking beautiful. Not in the trashy way of the patch bunnies who flocked to the Kings.

Swearing under my breath, I took the right toward the cemetery. I caught the flash of fabric in the rear-view and reached back, snatched her dress where it'd come loose, and tucked it back under her leg.

When I glanced in the mirror again, she was staring at me, her lips slightly parted and her eyes bright. If my fingers lingered too long, I'd blame it on that look.

The closer to the cemetery, the greener it got. As if the caretakers were fighting against the desert's invasion by planting shrubbery and grass that died in patches here and there. I felt like that grass, pieces of myself turning brown under the burn of expectations.

Everyone wanted something from me now. Even Riley, even if she didn't realize it yet. She was out of her element, someone had to look after her. I owed Archer that much.

But I had no idea what the fuck I was going to do without him. I hadn't planned for this, hadn't thought this far ahead. I didn't trust Preacher to keep the Desert Kings afloat the way Archer had. He was too fucking selfish.

As planned, I steered the bike right up to the grave itself, killing the engine and coasting between headstones careful not to tread where the dead lay.

I glanced back at Riley as I leaned the bike on its kickstand. She was unbuckling the helmet, trying to look anywhere but at me. I made her nervous. That it turned me on made me an asshole.

I didn't fucking care.

***

No matter how hard I tried to focus on the casket draped with Archer's leathers, my gaze drifted back where Riley chose to stand beside, not sit on, the satin-roped blue chairs at graveside.

The dress was too big; she was too skinny. Had she eaten today, hell, in the last week? Probably not. And it wasn't my business. I shouldn't care. Yet, already I did. This overwhelming desire to protect her came from somewhere I didn't understand.

She was Archer's daughter. I owed him at least that, because I'd known him enough to know he loved her. That's why he'd stayed away.

I positioned myself away from her, on the very corner, with a view of everyone. I wanted to stand right beside her, put myself between her and all of them. Not because she seemed weak, not because Archer would want me to. But there was an itch to be close.

Get through the service and get her the hell out of Hayes County.

After the funeral, I was going to get stoned and lose myself in pussy. Forget all of this, forget her. My gaze took in the crowd, faces I knew, some I didn't, but plenty of willing groupies up for a night of debauchery. Then it landed right back on Riley.

All the rest, each one, bled into the next and they all became the same.

Except her.

Riley wasn't like that.

Fuck.

I coughed to keep from spitting the word out loud and rubbed a hand across my mouth. The stiff collar kept up his sermon, drowning on about shit Archer had never cared about.

I slammed my fists in my pockets and forced my eyes on the casket and nothing else. In less than twenty-four hours I was turned inside out like a horny teenager.

There wasn't time for that shit. Archer hadn't shot himself. I had no proof except for the sick, sinking sensation in my gut.

As the casket was lowered into the ground, each Patch dumped a shovel of dirt into the ground on top of it. Mine was last. A lone, dark cloud slid in front of the sun.

The weather was unseasonably cool, but without the sun, gooseflesh rippled across my arms.

I turned the shovel, the dry dirt tumbling on top of the rest. And that was that. I waited for the closure, the comfort, but it never came. The man under those shovels of dirt had shaped me into the man I was.

He'd given me the life I had. How did I say goodbye?

Someone took the shovel and slapped a hand on my back in comfort. To keep from jerking away, I lit a cigarette and took a drag.

This time when I looked at Riley, she was watching me. Her auburn hair glistened gold and red. There was an easy acceptance on her face, like she realized this was my place to grieve more than hers. And for that, I could never hate her, no matter how much easier it would make things.

A loud, cracking bang echoed across the cemetery. Everyone ducked, some people half-dropping to the ground. Everyone except Riley, who stood holding Archer's folded cut and looking around, confused.

She didn't even have the good sense to shield herself from the sound of gunfire. I'd taken a full step before I stopped myself from going over and telling her off for not being smarter, more—*Fuck.*

Riley Bowman wasn't meant for my world. Archer had always known it.

Five

Riley

During the burial, for a brief second, there'd been an innocence to Cam that left my heart aching. He'd lost someone he cared about; the pain was etched in every feature. His mouth formed a rigid, unwavering line, like if he said a single word he'd shatter.

I wanted to go to him, apologize for intruding on his grief, and would have, but he stormed off, long legs eating up the yellow grass until he made it back to my father's bike. There was a rumble, a pop, and then nothing but a roar as he tore off out of the cemetery.

I still wore his flannel and would have waved after him to give it back—but my father's vest was heavy in my arms.

"You good?" AP sidled next to me on legs that bowed slightly at the knees.

Compared to the controlling and almost combative way Preacher stood near me during the funeral, and the sheer intensity of Cam, AP was cool like a brief respite from the sun.

"Yeah. Will the limo take me back home?"

AP gave a solemn nod. "Or anywhere else you want to go."

When he started toward the car, I went with him. It seemed natural to hang out beside him. He wore a pale gray dress shirt beneath his vest, rolled up to the elbows.

There were flickers of tattoos on his arms, which only made his vibe cooler.

"You were close to him?" I'd seen some photos in the hallway, so I already knew the answer.

He stopped short with a sad smile. "He was my best friend."

We walked quietly all the way to the limo, where he opened the door and squeezed my shoulder with the other hand. "If you ever want to know about him, call me."

Emotion stung the back of my eyes and burned in my nose, so I ducked into the car. Before he could shut me in, a feminine form pushed past. Dylan, an apologetic smile on her face, crawled in with me. "I rode over in the limo, so I don't have a ride back."

I patted the seat beside me. "The company is appreciated." I liked her. Unlike most of the other women there, she wasn't sizing me up. There'd been so many of them, sliding in and out of leather clad bikers, climbing on the backs of bikes, each one more bitter and angry looking than the next.

Dylan waited until we pulled from the graveyard before talking. "Must feel like you're on an island all alone, with sharks circling."

"Sort of, yeah." My shoulders relaxed and sank more comfortably against the seat. I picked at some gold thread on one of the patches.

"They're curious." She gazed out the window. "I didn't even know Archer had a kid...most didn't."

"In a way, neither did I." That he was out there somewhere, yes. But anything about him, no. He was the man who ruined Mom's life, who kept her looking over her shoulder all the time. He was dangerous, all bikers were.

She chuckled, the sound warm and inviting. "I'm glad you're here, at least. I... always felt sad he was alone, since..." She choked up a bit and swallowed.

Her emotion hit me in a way similar to Cam's. I leaned across and squeezed her hand. "I wish..." I'd what, come sooner? Known him? That he wouldn't have spent the rest of his life alone since my mom left. "From where I'm sitting, he was never alone. I'm sorry for your loss."

She caught my gaze and held it. Her eyes were so bright with tears they reminded me of the way the ocean reflected the sky, crystalline blue. The moisture making everything more vivid. There was something there that hadn't been before, as if for the first time we really saw each other. "Thank you."

"Want to come with me to the clubhouse? There's a celebration of life thing, lots of pictures and stuff, maybe even some stories about Archer." She was sharing something with me, a part of their world—to help me understand.

I wanted to hug her. Instead, I gripped the sides of the leather. "I'd like that."

She smiled and called to the driver that there was a change of plans.

***

Dylan said to wear whatever I felt the most comfortable in. I opted for skinny jeans, a pair of well-loved Vans, and a red shirt with short sleeves.

In my father's kitchen, I hesitated. Dylan waited in the limo. I could stop whatever charade this was, hide away in the spare bedroom, and wait for the next few weeks to pass quietly. Hide, like the frightened rabbit Mom had been, but I'd already done that. It hadn't saved her or me.

I could learn about the man whose death had brought me here. These people loved him. Would I have? Had she been wrong? I'd never know if I hid. It was time to do the one thing I hadn't: *live*.

On my way out the door, I collected Cam's flannel and ran my fingers over the worn leather I'd hung on the back of the chair. Cam had loved Archer, and from everything I'd seen Archer had loved him too.

I thought of the pain on Cam's face; of the quiet way he'd stood from the crowd. I was intruding on his grief by being here. If I could give him the peace of my leaving, I would. But if I did—

The room spun a little as I remembered the hole life had dug for me. That it was caving in, similar to the dirt they'd piled on top of Archer's casket. I couldn't leave, had to wait it out just like the letter said. This was my only shot. If I left there was no home to go to, no future, nothing.

***

The clubhouse was a metal and brick building stuck out in the middle of the desert, sheltered by reddish rock formations on one side and mountains in the back. One half of it was two stories, industrial with faded metal siding, and the other side was topped with a giant neon sign humming: Desert Kings Motorcycle Club.

Bikes, chrome shimmering in the fading sunlight, stretched as far as I could see and people spilled out into the barren desert lot beside the building. A stage had been erected there, and a band played. This was unlike any wake or memorial I'd ever attended.

When I opened the limo door, I was assaulted with the mixed rumbling sounds of motorcycles and bluesy rock. The scent of smoked meats made my stomach rumble.

I clutched my stomach with Cam's shirt and Dylan grinned. "Come on inside. I'll get you some food before I get changed."

The clubhouse was laid out how I'd imagined a biker bar would be. There was another stage here, where a young woman strummed a guitar and sang like her best friend had died. There was a gleaming copper topped bar, glass shelves covered in liquor bottles, and a mirrored bar back.

Tables had been pushed away from the center of the large space to make room for my dad's bike. The warm engine still made tinkling, popping sounds as it cooled. Behind the Harley was a table filled with pictures and mementos of Archer Bowman.

"Riley? This is Kenna." Dylan gestured to the petite young woman, no older than me, perched on a barstool. Her dark hair was threaded with neon pink and twisted on top of her head in a messy bun. She wore khaki shorts with black Doc Martins and an off the shoulder band shirt tied up in the back.

"Hi!" She hopped off the stool and stood barely as tall as my chest, with more energy than I could ever muster. "I'll grab you a plate. Whatcha drinking?"

"Whatever she wants… give her the damn bottle!" Preacher appeared behind me, eyes red from weed or liquor, I couldn't be sure. I'd hoped to see Cam before having to deal with the older man again. No such luck.

Something about him made me feel dirty. His lips were wet, greasy as he rubbed them together beneath the handlebar mustache, as if he were contemplating me in a way that instantly made me want distance between us.

I made some, climbing onto a stool several feet away as Dylan headed toward a set of stairs on the other side of the bar.

Though he made like he wanted to talk, he didn't get a chance to, as another big biker threw his arm around his neck and pulled him away. My body relaxed in relief, and I turned to Kenna, who waited patiently.

"What'll it be?" When she smiled, freckles danced across the bridge of her nose. The effect was cute and made me want to like her. Many of the women I'd seen so far were devoid of any such personality. The life hadn't been sucked out of her yet.

Once, when I was about fifteen, I'd sneaked a mango margarita one of Mom's friends had left on the table at a pool party. But this didn't seem like the place to ask for a blended drink. I'd never been a huge partier, but what the hell. "Tequila."

She turned, the dark mess of hair wiggling atop her head. "This one." The bottle looked expensive, adorned with a green ribbon and cork stopper. She slid it to me and disappeared into a kitchen and smacked a small shot glass onto the copper bar top.

My eyes were drawn to the mirror, allowing me to see behind me. A small crowd had formed around Archer's bike. A motley crew of bikers with bottles and glasses in their hands. Past them, a familiar form had stopped Dylan at the foot of the stairs.

Cam was leaned into her, his brow furrowed as he talked and the muscles on his tattooed arm tensed as he gripped the stair-rail with both hands. The two stood close enough to be intimate, and a small fire of jealousy flared to life in my gut.

Dylan frowned, and her lips tightened in apparent annoyance. She pulled away and mouthed something that made the lines on his forehead deepen, right before she held up a parting middle finger.

I looked away, half ashamed of my tingle of relief, as he made his way toward the bar.

"She keeps clothes upstairs. Several of us do." Kenna laid a plate filled to overflowing in front of me. "When we work the bar, makes it easier to get cleaned up. There are a few bedrooms up there and if I'm being honest...I'd only use those bathrooms. None of the guys ever do." She winked, like sharing some amusing secret.

Having never lived with any men, I took her word for it.

I ate with as much dignity as a starving woman could. I hadn't eaten real food in weeks. The brisket and ribs were the best thing I'd put in my mouth in years. After several bites, I popped the cork out of the tequila and took a swallow. It scalded all the way down, but I didn't sputter or flinch.

In truth, the burn felt good. Being here did.

"This your first time in Dry Valley?" she asked.

I nodded, swallowed another pork filled bite, and wiped my mouth. "My first time in Nevada."

"As you've noticed, not really a lot to see." She giggled and grinned, dimples accenting her cheeks. "Unless you've got a thing for hot bikers."

She pointed across the bar, to a guy with the sides of his head shaved, but a ponytail at the base of his neck. The bare sides of his head were tattooed with thick, dark ink.

"That one's mine." She turned her wrist where she wore a leather bracelet with the word Ghost stitched in. "I'm officially Ghost's old lady or I will be when he's patched in."

"You aren't a day over twenty-one or I'll eat my fist." I made a face and she giggled.

Her laugh grew to a full belly chuckle. "It doesn't have anything to do with age, just means I'm his girl. His woman, ya know?"

Sounded like a bunch of patriarchal bullshit. "Got it." I took another swig before digging back into my food.

"I don't think your daddy ever had an old lady, not that I saw. My momma dated a King for a while when I was young. When she left, I stayed with him. Was your mama a—"

"You talk too much, Kenna." Cam's voice slipped over my senses, much like the tequila. Two tatted, lean arms propped on the copper top beside me, before Cam reached over and took my bottle and a long swig of it.

Kenna blinked, sucked in a deep breath, and quickly found somewhere else to be. He lifted his brow, and my eyes followed the way his throat moved when he swallowed. Why was everything he did so sexy?

I snatched my bottle away.

"That was rude." I gestured toward an obviously offended Kenna, who had scampered off to her boyfriend.

"She'll get over it." He glowered at me. He opened his mouth, like he had something to say, but paused before saying it. Maybe softening his words before he spoke. "Why didn't you go back to the house?"

What he meant was: *Why are you here?* I didn't have an answer for that, not one that was easy to explain. Especially not with over six feet of sexy as hell biker bearing down on me.

That he was that hot just wasn't fair.

This isn't your world.

I took a swig of the tequila and nodded toward Archer's bike. It was easier to think of him like that. My father felt weird. Rick was too formal. "I don't know. Dylan offered and I thought maybe..." I let my voice trail off as I got caught up in his blue gaze. The pain I'd seen there, the vulnerability he'd had graveside, was gone. Instead, I found an arrogant, sexy edge that told me he'd leave me naked and begging for more.

"Like I told your ignorant ass, she deserves to know who he was." The ire dripped from every one of Dylan's words. She hopped onto the stool beside me, dressed in high rise jeans that flared around cowboy boots and a cropped, black corset top.

What I'd give to have curves like that.

Cam merely flicked her a glance and pushed a hand through his dirty blond hair, unaffected. "Let me know if you need anything." He pushed away from the bar and turned to leave.

"Cam, wait." I spun in my stool, hopping off so fast I fell against him as he stopped and turned.

The leather of the vest was cool, but the rest of his chest was warm. His fingers too, as they caught my elbow to keep me from tumbling forward.

"Here, I brought this back." I pushed the flannel between us, a cotton buffer between the weird tingling sensation running across my body and him.

"Thanks." His grin was slow, unexpected, and so hot it stole my breath.

He took the shirt and released me like I had the plague before walking off without a word.

"Is it all women he has an issue with, or just me?" I asked breathlessly to no one in particular.

Dylan barked a laugh and waved Kenna back over. "Honestly, he's a good guy. Archer's death...hit him hard. He was like—"

"A father to him?" I finished for her. I'd already seen as much, just being in Archer's house.

She closed her eyes tight for a moment, like she was blinking back tears that never came.

I could understand that. He didn't know me. I was here, imposing myself on his life during a dark time. I understood about those.

With a sigh, I glanced from the tequila to the plate of food and chose the tequila.

Six

RILEY

"We're all family." Dylan walked me around Archer's bike. An old, faded vest lay draped across the handlebars. Very similar to the one I'd been given.

"That looks like…"

A striking, rangy man approached. Attractive with tattoos up to his chin, and blond hair cut short on the sides but pulled back in a tight, high ponytail. "His original cut." He tossed a tatted-up arm over Dylan's shoulder and kissed the top of her head.

"Love you, Dee."

"I know." She stopped, seemingly caught between beaming up at him and giving him a hard shove.

I chuckled. They knew each other well.

"Another brother?"

She shook her head and shrugged his arm off. He stumbled with more drama than necessary before catching himself. "No, this is Jester."

He made a mock bow, with a grandiose gesture of his free arm. The other clutched a dark beer bottle. Import. Fancy.

On one side of his neck, a full house of hearts was splayed across like a winning hand on a table. Across his throat, fire and smoke, and on the other side, a demonic jester face. The tattoos blending together seamlessly.

When he caught me looking, he grinned and nodded to a corner of the bar where a clean, clinical tattoo station was set up. The man who sat there didn't just have wide shoulders but rippling muscles that bulged from the t-shirt he wore. At first glance, he looked older. But he wasn't. Behind the beard, the face was young, barely thirty, if that.

The woman on the chair in front of him, her hip being worked on, was much older. The contrast was interesting.

"Puck did everything up here." Jester waved at his throat. "Got a shop in town, nice place. If you want any ink, check him out. Because you're Archer's kid, you'll get one hell of a discount."

I'd never thought of a tattoo. But the tequila was making a lot of things seem like good ideas. I searched the room and saw Cam standing with Dylan's brother. He was laughing, his face bright. *That's new.* All I'd seen was his brooding side. This was equal parts attractive and disarming.

To keep from thinking of all the ways I found Cam attractive, even after he'd basically assaulted me, I focused on Dylan's brother instead. His dark hair hung shaggy over his ears and too long on his neck but not long enough to tie back like Jester's. Were it not for the dark hair covering his jaw and chin, he'd be gorgeous. Maybe he was even with it.

A warmth spread out over my chest when I turned and got caught in Cam's blueish gaze. He held me frozen as Jester and Dylan talked around me. I couldn't move. All I could do was look at him and think of...things I shouldn't. More bad ideas.

I shivered and blinked, breaking the moment.

"That one I'll claim." Dylan bumped me with her shoulder. "Got eyes for Jace?"

"Merc." Jester interjected and took a swig of beer. "Her and every other chick in here."

He pointed at Cam. "Or maybe Savage."

I must have made a face, because he laughed. "It's his name. Seriously, but my man lives up to it."

"Not surprising." I'd experienced a small amount of his fierceness.

"Don't scare her off when she's got to sleep at Archer's. It's *not* going to make her run to your place instead." Dylan gave Jester a gentle kick to the shin.

"Is this the face of someone who would do such a thing?" He batted his lashes, feigning innocence.

"One hundred percent." I laughed, more at ease than I had been in months. Maybe it was the company, but I was betting it was the tequila. Somewhere, my mom was telling me not to let my guard down—to get out of there.

He conceded with a wink.

Needing the conversation to be about anything other than Cam, I brushed my fingers over the worn patch that read Archer on the chest of the original vest. "He started the club, right?"

"Yeah. Him, AP, and Preacher were the first official three." This time, he slung his arm around my shoulders. He rattled off names I would never remember. "They all came later."

I expected him to smell like gasoline and stale cigarettes. But he didn't. There was a woodsy, clean scent and his touch was companionable, lulling me into an even bigger sense of calm and comfort.

No warning bells.

"Let me take you on a tour." Jester steered me to a well-lit hallway behind the stairs.

He dropped his arm when we rounded the corner. The walls were lined with pictures and framed leather vests, even a flag or two. Two large, wooden doors dominated the end of the hall. The Desert King MC insignia—a skull with piston crossbones and a crooked crown—burned into them.

"Archer and AP rode dirt bikes together growing up, followed along behind a bunch of outlaw motorcycle clubs in southern Cali. Archer served a few tours in the middle east, then came back and decided he needed space and freedom but missed the brotherhood. He collected some guys, came here, built bikes, and sold weed. The MC was born from that."

Which one was which, I wondered, searching the faded image of several men of various ages. Jester gestured with a long, nimble finger, with dark lines soaked into the skin. He pointed to a tall man, older than the others, all the way to the left. "Goat. Got creamed by a semi when I was first patched in." Then to the man beside him. "AP."

"He could never deny Merc." His father could have been his double, save for the devilish grin. When Merc did smile, it was like he wasn't sure he was doing it right.

"Yup."

He moved down the wall a few paces and nodded to another image. This one less faded and without the orange hue. Brighter, three young men all in vests, laughing together. I recognized AP and Archer, but the other...

"Who?"

"Preacher. Before he got fat." He sniggered. "Archer brought him back with them from the desert."

I took another swallow of tequila and leaned a little closer to Jester who placed the tips of the fingers of his freehand against the small of my back. Unlike when Preacher had touched me, this was light and companionable. I didn't feel like I should be jerking away.

He was attractive, but in a different way than Cam. Both dangerous, but Jester more agreeable.

"Are a lot of the guys ex-military?"

"Yeah, some of them." He tossed his bottle into a trashcan behind us and took my tequila for a long swig before making a face.

"Any of the younger guys military, too?"

He shook his head. "Well, Merc was for a little while. Coincidentally, if you need any guns—for the zombie apocalypse or whatever—he's your man."

"Zombies?"

"Yup." He laughed and handed me back my bottle. "Hey, our government has been known to do some weird shit. I'm convinced Area Fifty-One isn't aliens at all."

There were worse things than being prepared. Amused, I moved to a group of pictures on a table beside the double doors. These pictures were more official. Five men hovered around a large oak table. The picture tinted almost brown and faded. Then six, the faces changing—some aging, some new. I followed them all the way to the most current.

My father was there, at the head of that table. So were AP, Preacher, Cam, Merc, and Jester.

"The table," he said, as if that told me everything I needed to know.

"What's that mean?"

"Officers, governing body of the Desert Kings." He puffed up, full of pride. "I'm Road Captain."

"That makes you something special, huh?" I teased and thumped him on his chest, though I had no idea what he was talking about.

"I mean..." He wiped at something invisible on his shoulder and preened a little. "If you're ever of the mind to find out, I could take you for a ride sometime."

"Or not." The voice from the end of the hall was so cold the temperature dropped twenty degrees.

Jester whistled long and low, and I hugged the bottle to my chest.

Cam leaned against the door frame and jerked his chin back out in the main part of the clubhouse. I wanted to shout at him. The past fifteen or so minutes had been the most fun I'd had in weeks. I opened my mouth, shut it, and managed to glare at him.

Jester wasn't bothered at all. He chuckled and strolled down the hall. Smacking Cam on the shoulder as he went.

Cam watched him quietly before making his way toward me. I ducked away, focusing on the pictures, to keep from watching the way the black t-shirt bunched and shifted as he walked.

"That was rude." I tried to bite back the comment. I was intruding on his world, but it didn't give him the right to act like he could tell me what to do.

"Was it?" He said unbothered, from behind me.

I could feel him there, though he didn't touch me. The prickling awareness radiated all around me, clanging like warning bells. I'd flirted with guys before, but it hadn't felt like this. Would I flirt with Cam or just melt at his feet like the groupies that hovered all around the clubhouse?

"It was." I doubled down, focused on my annoyance to ignore the attraction.

I took another swig of tequila. It would have been better with some orange slices, maybe even a lime, but the burn down my throat strengthened me. The warmth of my buzz chased away anything else and left me strong enough to turn to face him.

"You sure that's what you're into?"

Jester was handsome, tattoos and all. Sure, he didn't quite compare to Cam, but...

"I could be."

He leaned closer, so that his goatee tickled against my ear. "If you want to get a little kinky...that's one thing, darlin. But that shit?" He slipped his hand up until it wrapped around my throat. He didn't squeeze, but his meaning was clear.

Trembling, more from his touch than anything, I met his blue gaze.

"I didn't think so." He grinned and let go. "But I bet you'd look hot all tied up in that throne of his."

I blinked twice and chased him back the way he had come.

"Wait, what? A throne?"

His laugh was easy and warm, something I hadn't expected. "He's very proud of it."

"Holy shit." I took another sip and shook my head. "You're right. Not for me."

He spun, walking backwards, his brow raised and, for the first time for me, an easy smile on his face. "Believe me, darlin, I know. That's why I intervened."

I twisted my lips and narrowed my gaze. "So that's what the asshole vibe is all about. You're looking out for me."

He stopped at the doorway. "I haven't been a dick to you."

Not entirely true. "But..." I let that trail off without agreeing.

With a flustered sigh, he rubbed a hand over his mouth.

"You don't like me. I get it." The tequila hampered my ability to staunch the flow of words. "I show up out of nowhere, mess up everything you've got going on. I'm sorry. Really, I am. I want to be here even less than you want me here."

"Stop." He looked down at his feet and mumbled something about too much, but I missed it. "Let me show you something."

He started up the stairs, when I didn't immediately follow, he glanced over his shoulder. "Should I be offended that you'll go into a dead-end hallway with Jester, but not up a flight of stairs with me?"

I looked back to where Jester was cutting up with several others, including Dylan. "He's nice."

"For fuck's sake." Cam spat and rolled his eyes toward the ceiling.

Both amused and curious enough, I followed him.

Seven

CAM

Cam

The rooftop of the clubhouse was my safe place. I didn't have to pretend here. All around us, the party spread out into the parking lot and beyond. The band was back on stage, lights and rigging were an explosion of color on the desert.

But nothing as shocking to the system as the woman who walked out onto the roof with me.

"Wow."

"Told you." I walked to the edge, looking over the other part of the party. Groups of people gathered around bonfires. Some on bikes, others in chairs. I could name about half of them. The rest came from other charters, most had known Archer.

In the west, the sun had sunk so low only a pale orange glow kissed the purple sky. Archer would have loved this shit. There was a reason he'd bought this place, built the clubhouse here.

"Beautiful." Her face was serene again, like she was soaking up everything.

"Yeah." Shouldn't be surprising that his daughter noticed the sky, too. I looked away, out toward the rock formations, one of my favorite rides.

The music was loud, but up here it was bearable. I could think clearly, try to remember why I wanted her close.

"They're pretty good." She made small talk when I said nothing.

"Not my thing."

"What is? Gangster rap?" She tapped her chin with the tip of the bottle. "You don't look like you'd go for country."

I curled my lip and jerked a chin toward the stage. "Whatever it is, it ain't *that*."

She chuckled and walked over to one of two folding chairs. The one she chose was well worn. Ironic, that the last person to sit there had been Archer.

I flexed my fingers and made a fist. Holding her throat, even for just a second, had left me caught between feeling like a fucking barbarian and hornier than a teenager with his first porn video.

I sat in the other chair and kicked my feet up onto the short ledge.

"This your spot?"

I pursed my lips and nodded. "Something like that." It was Archer's spot, but I'd found myself up here more in the past week than I had in years. She was right. She was intruding on my life. Yet, each time she poked her head in, I opened the god-damned door. Like right now.

Annoyed with myself more than her, I jerked out a cigarette and lit it. Even the nicotine couldn't chase away the edge that had sharpened since Archer died. I doubt anything could. I wanted to cuss, to kick something. She shouldn't be here.

We sat in silence for a long time, music and shouts from the party cutting through the night air. A woman's shrill giggle, more laughter. All sounds of a good time, of happy people. Not very much grieving—but it was meant to be a celebration. It pissed me off.

"You don't want me here, do you?"

Did I? "Haven't decided yet."

She laughed, then covered her mouth as if she hadn't meant to. It was endearing and made me fight against a grin.

"I'm not trying to invade your space or hijack your grief. I feel like I'm this great big reminder of something. Only, I don't know what any of it is." The tequila made her chattier. It was weirdly soothing.

"Why's that?"

"I didn't know him." Her words were slurring a little, and her eyes were heavy, even in the shadow of the lights from below. "I just show up out of nowhere. I could be anyone, you don't know me. Haven't met me."

But I'd seen her more times than she'd ever known. Archer had kept close tabs on her.

"Money is a great motivator." I tried to keep my voice level, hide the judgment. She wasn't my problem. Keeping her safe was. I had no proof, not yet. Just a gut feeling. But it was one I couldn't ignore. There was that edge again, flint racing across it, making it sharper.

A familiar old anger boiled up inside me. A feeling I'd put away years ago, locked up tight. It threatened to take over. When I reached to her, she handed me the bottle. I took two deep swallows before gulping in the cool night air, to fend off the burn in my nostrils.

She turned toward me, her eyes narrowed, before shrugging. "Screw it. My mom raised me on her own. Archer was never there. I was pre-law before Mom got sick. Left to take care of her, couldn't work because we couldn't afford daily care..." She drew in a shaky breath.

I curled my fingers around the bottle to keep from what—holding her hand? That was some bullshit.

Still needing movement, I handed her the bottle. She rolled it in her hands a few times.

"I lost the house and had to give her a beggar's funeral. Everything else that's left is in storage in California."

"Where'd you go?"

She put the bottle down, stood, and walked to the edge, moving like she was running away from the truth. I'd done that a lot the past few weeks.

"Moved into my car. Do you know, twenty-four-hour gyms are a homeless girl's best friend? Cheap membership, well-lit parking lots, and free showers. But the cops occasionally chase you off and your choices are crack motels or creepy truck stops."

Jesus. Archer hadn't known, couldn't have...if he had, he would have done something about it.

"Riley..."

"Do *not.*" Her voice trembled with the tears. "I can't stand it when people feel sorry for me."

I held up my hands in surrender, shoved them into my pockets, and followed her to the edge. I'd been homeless before, slept here as a matter of fact, until Archer helped me. He should have helped her.

"How long?"

"Three or four months. I started a job right before this but..." She closed her eyes. "Boss is a pervert."

My sympathy evaporated in a cloud of anger. I'd find out who he was and break all his fingers if he'd touched her.

She glanced up at me and tilted her head, eyes still watery and sad. "What are you thinking?"

I blinked and frowned. "What are you talking about?"

"Your face just—" she waved a hand in front of her face and then back up. "—for a minute, your eyes get so dark and there's nothing there. You've done it a few times since I met you."

"Trust me, you don't want to know." I snorted.

That was a part of me she never needed to meet. No one did. That darkness was always right there, ready to seep in, hungry to make me do bad things all over again.

"You keep telling me that, and I might believe it." She turned back toward the party. "And you're right. When I checked the PO Box this week, there was a letter and a check. Some lawyer saying I needed to be here for the funeral and reading of the will, and if I was, there was more money waiting for me."

Why the fuck would Archer want her here, knowing how volatile things were? Keep her safe her entire life and then throw her to the lions after his murder. What in the actual fuck had he been thinking?

He probably didn't think he'd get killed. He damn sure didn't pull the trigger himself.

"Yeah, I'm the bitch who just showed up for money." She walked away. "I'll go."

"Stop." I took her by the arm before she could walk off. "Who was the lawyer?"

"Kimbrell and something?"

We have a winner. "Yeah, that's right. It's your money, darlin." And there's a fuck-ton more than that, really. Or should be, if what he told me was true. "Everything today, Archer planned before he died. We all do. Who rode his bike, where his daughter sat, everything. He wanted you here, you are here. End of story."

"But *you* don't want me here."

I tossed my head back and rubbed my hand over my mouth and the hair on my chin. No, I didn't want her here. But not for any of the reasons she thought. I couldn't tell her that, though, not until I knew more.

"What I want doesn't matter."

"It does to me." Her voice was so quiet it was almost a squeak.

All the blood in my head rushed straight down to my crotch, and I cursed as I turned away. I, for damn sure, didn't need to want her. *Fuck.*

"Beating the guys off of Archer's daughter is a pain in the ass, but there are worse things."

It was her turn to blink, shocked. I couldn't help it; I laughed. "Darlin, every man in this place is circling you like a shark. You're new, different, and unattainable. Why do you think Jester was sneaking off with you? You can't *really think* he wanted to give you the history of the club."

"Oh." She turned away, blushing.

And then she made a noise in her throat, half choking, half gasp. "Are they...?"

I looked down at a chair beneath us, a good bit away from the others. I couldn't be sure who it was, but a woman was bouncing on top of a charter member. "Yup." Then I snorted. "One less shark to worry about."

She laughed and leaned her head on my shoulder.

The desire that gripped me was enough I had to focus out on the rocks. I remembered all the shit Archer had done for me. The lessons he taught, but more importantly, the secrets he kept. "Listen, if the house isn't yours, he'll have left it to the club. Either way, it belongs to you as long as you want it. As long as it takes, cool?"

At least there, I could keep an eye on her.

"Yeah, thanks." She nodded.

She was quiet and leaned against me for so long I thought she'd passed out. Then she whispered. "You said every man here."

"Yup."

"Even you?"

I bit back the groan. Fuck yes, I was one of them. She didn't give off the damsel in distress vibe; she came here to fix shit for herself. I could admire that. It made her sexier than hell.

I needed to put space between us, fast.

"Come on, darlin, let's get you home."

Eight

RILEY

An energetic knocking broke through the cocoon of sleep that wrapped around me. I was warm and comfy, snuggled down in a bed that smelled of clean sheets.

My bed is in storage.

Something weighed my brain down, made it hard to wake. I didn't want to get up, or to acknowledge that I needed to be awake. For the first time in months, I was warm, safe.

My eyes flew open. Several terrified seconds ticked by as I placed the pale blue paint and Americana art on the walls. I was in Archer's guest room. The foggy bliss was the remainder of the alcohol in my system.

The limo brought me back, and I'd stumbled in here, leaving my shoes and jeans somewhere in the kitchen, my shirt on the floor by the bed. I'd barely managed to tug on a t-shirt before passing out.

I stood, stretched, and the knocking sounded again.

"Crap." I jerked a pair of shorts from my bag and hopped into them.

My heart raced, but not from fear. As I rounded the corner, it slowed. Cam wouldn't need to knock, would he?

Dylan waved through the glass, holding up a brown bag with a smile on her face and dark sunglasses hiding her eyes.

"Morning," she said as I let her in, dark ponytail swinging behind her. "I come bearing pastries and coffee." She dropped the bag, and I peeked inside as she went back out.

Croissants, the chocolate filled kind, and several types of Danish.

"Just save one of the cherry ones or Savage will get all in my ass." She brought in a tray with four foam cups.

"I like mocha, I got you one too. That okay?" She plucked one out and handed it to me.

"Perfect." I settled in at the table as she moved around the kitchen, opening and closing cabinets until she found some plates and put them on the table.

In the distance, the hum of a motorcycle crept closer until it became a wall shaking roar up the driveway and reverberated in the carport. The sound drowned out the fluttering of the butterflies that kicked up in my chest.

When Dylan handed me a plate and napkin, I dug out a croissant. And another bike pulled in behind Cam's.

"My brother." She shrugged and sat beside me. "They both ended up crashing at the clubhouse last night."

Having seen the slew of willing women there, that didn't surprise me. But I didn't like the ugly little feeling nestled in my stomach.

Cam came in first, Merc right behind him. Dylan's brother was prettier than I remembered. His dark hair framing his handsome face. He wasn't as tense here; the edge gone. The half-grin was natural, easy.

Cam took the cup Dylan offered and stopped short of digging through the bag, his gaze landing on Archer's leather vest, neatly folded over the chair under the old land-line phone on the wall. There was that momentary flash of vulnerability usually hidden beneath the surface. The grief, as his daughter, I should feel.

The bite of chocolate croissant in my mouth soured, and I placed it back on the plate and chased the nausea inducing bite with sweet latte.

"I still can't believe he's gone." Dylan's tone was forlorn.

Merc grunted, though there was a gentleness to the sound as he hopped onto the counter and pulled a bag of weed from his pocket, breaking it up to stuff a cigar shell.

Cam said nothing, instead ran a hand through his hair and sat down, digging into the bag and pulling out a cherry Danish.

He looked over the edge of the bag and caught me watching him. His lifted brow held a touch of arrogance challenging me. To what, I didn't know. I flicked my gaze to my lap.

Or maybe you do.

Dylan mentioned something about the party the night before, changing the subject, though I missed most of what she said. I found it increasingly difficult to focus when Cam was around. Especially when he seemed edgy and pissed off, like now.

His deep rumble joined the fray, and something broke free in my chest. These three, they loved each other. They were comfortable here. This was the family Archer created when he'd left me behind.

You don't belong here.

Forgetting my hangover, I stood so fast my head spun. But I clutched the back of the chair long enough to steady myself before walking out. I'd made it as far as the guest bedroom when Cam caught up.

"What's up?" He started from the doorway, lifting a hand like he was going to reach for me. A battle waged in his expression. Concern softening his eyes and something else, something darker hardening the line of his mouth. He was caught between wanting to comfort me and not trusting me.

"I ...." My voice came out in a croak and I ducked into the tiny half bath and locked the door. Once there, I let the emotion wash over me.

My life was shit. Any dreams or desires, any plans I'd made, were long gone. I was just some piece of desert white trash sleeping in her car. That's where I belonged. Not here, intruding on their grief.

Fuck.

The hot water beat down on me, each scalding drop washing away more of my self-pity. I'd tried so hard to be good my entire life. Maybe if I was, my dad would come find me. Maybe if I'd been smarter, my life would be better. Maybe if I'd tried just a little harder—Mom wouldn't have died.

These people didn't know me, wouldn't understand what it was like to be alone, lost. They had their connections to each other, some of them since birth. I had nothing. No one. Not even a memory of my dead father. What had been a sad day for them, had been one of the happiest I'd had since Mom's diagnosis. I was a trespasser here, but part of me didn't want to leave.

The other part wanted to run like hell.

I don't know how long I stayed in the shower, but I heard the guys move outside talking near the bathroom window. Probably going up to Cam's or the garage.

When I opened the door, I found Dylan sitting on the freshly made bed, crisscross applesauce with a photo album in her lap.

"The guys are outside, smoking," she said, and then glanced up at me with a hesitant smile. "You looked like you needed a friend."

"Thanks, I think?" I fumbled, before busying myself with my suitcase and clinging to the towel wrapped around me.

At least it was Dylan in the room waiting for me, not Cam. The blush crept hotly up my neck.

"You should unpack, you know." She nodded toward the suitcase I stood beside. "Archer wanted you to stay, or he wouldn't have set things up this way."

But he'd never tried to see me, never been a father to me the way he had to Cam. And how much did I tell her? I had a brief recollection of opening up to Cam, telling him where I'd come from. Sick to my stomach, I clutched a hand there. "I don't know."

I considered hiding in the bathroom again but turned my back to her and put on my clothes.

As I changed, Dylan continued companionably. "I checked the laundry room. There's detergent and stuff. If you find anything else you need, I can go get it for you."

"I can get what I need. But I appreciate the offer."

When I finished, she patted the bed beside her. "Come here, I know Jester gave you a bit of a rundown yesterday. I figured you'd want the real story."

I sat and listened as she told me about Archer and AP, and their brotherhood that started when they were in diapers. Only children, best friends. Archer had been the best man at her parents' wedding.

"What happened to her?" I pointed at the pretty woman with brownish hair who reminded me a lot of Dylan, especially in the flare of her hips and slope of her sleepy eyes.

"She lives outside of Vegas. They divorced when I was a kid. Jace and I lived with her until we were teenagers. I was always a daddy's girl, so when Jace moved to Dry Valley, I did too."

"I was a royal bitch when I was younger. Thought I was queen bee around here." Dylan's chuckle lured me in, put me at ease.

"I imagine you still are."

"Nah," her voice changed, almost resigned now, "I learned really quick that there isn't a queen here. It's a boys' club. Our job is to stay out of the way and not ask questions."

And it was obvious she wasn't happy about it.

There were pictures of a younger Dylan, one even of a bunch of teenagers in a smoky room, Dylan curled up in Cam's lap, his hand very comfortable between her thighs. I wasn't jealous, couldn't be...not with how she'd treated me since I'd got here. But I couldn't help but meet her gaze, surprised.

This time, her raspy laugh was full bodied, and she fell back on the bed. "God, that was so long ago. We were young, stupid kids. It didn't work, for a bunch of reasons."

Her blue eyes were bright with laughter. "Damn, we were teenagers. Nobody else really thinks of it anymore. I don't. I doubt he does."

"You've never hooked up since?" Maybe I was more than a little jealous.

"Hell no. To be honest, we only messed around." She sat back up, wiping at tears with the back of her hand. "Cam was more about quantity over quality back then."

Then she grew somber. "Cam's always been running from something. I'm not sure what it is. I don't even think my brother knows. It made him...different."

He was, indeed.

"What about the rest?"

"Of the guys?" She brightened a little. "The best of them is Puck. Don't let the name throw you. He's not some Shakespearean wanna be. He played minor league hockey for a few years. The name stuck because of that. He's a single dad, works hard, bleeds Desert King gold."

There was a softness and love in her voice when she spoke of all of them. Dylan served as my deeper introduction to people I'd barely shaken hands with. Even laughing when I told her about the situation in the tribute hall—as I'd learned it was called.

"Cam's VP now. Power trickles down from position to position. All the guys are supposed to do what he says outside of the table, unless Preacher says otherwise." When I looked confused, she explained further. "The MC governs itself, a sort of fuck you to the establishment. Patched members vote on officers who make decisions for the entire charter. And that's about all I know, because..." She gave me an exasperated look before continuing.

"Jester is Road Captain, so he's in charge of long rides. Dad is Treasurer. Drop Top is Secretary, my brother is Sergeant at Arms, Puck is Enforcer. There's usually a few at the table without titles, alternate delegates. Like Paul. He's new, voted to the table a few days ago."

"Puck enforces all the rules?" I couldn't see anyone forcing Cam Savage to do anything.

"Nah. Jace or one of Preacher's goons usually does that."

"Members really have to do whatever the officers say?" It seemed archaic but oddly sexy.

I thought of those two intricate wooden doors. Of Cam behind them, holding court. One seat away from President. "Cam told Jester to leave yesterday when he was with me, and he did."

"Probably a good thing—Jester is a freak." But she said it with a smile.

"Is there really a throne?" I asked the question I'd wanted to ask since Cam told me.

"Oh yeah. There's an entire sex dungeon at his house."

"You been in there?"

"No." She answered so quick we both burst into giggles. "He wishes. Again, I say—freak."

When she talked about them, everyone seemed so normal, and I felt more like I wasn't an outcast.

"You're wrong though," I said as I rolled up on an elbow. "I can't see you ever being a bitch."

"Not to you, not yet." She winked and swatted at my knee. "Now, let's go find these two assholes and see what we are doing today."

Nine

RILEY

Turns out we spent the day looking through Archer's stuff, like we did every day for the next week. I learned I enjoyed Merc and Dylan. She was easy to be around, and he had a gruff charm that was growing on me.

Cam was in and out. Mostly, he stayed away from me. It's like he'd sent the Merrick siblings to keep an eye out so he didn't have to. I was okay with that. The space made it possible for me to breathe, to process the lies my mom had constructed about Archer, and compare them to what I was learning each day. About the Desert Kings. About him. About this life.

By Saturday, Merc and Cam had moved to the garage, meticulously going through every toolbox, like they were searching for some sign of how to move on with the Kings without him.

The lawyer had put off reading the will, per the request of investigators. I found that odd, but I'd have to wait until we were alone and ask Cam. Which didn't seem likely to happen anytime soon.

Dylan and I went through closets, finding countless pictures, boxes of mementos, and a literal arsenal.

"What are we looking for?" I asked her from Archer's bedroom.

On the bed, we'd laid out at least a dozen guns. Ammunition piled up on the floor. Nervously, I'd made sure all of them were pointed away from me—just in case.

Dylan seemed to ignore the question, standing and surveying the weapons. "What in the actual fuck?"

"Jester said your brother prepares for zombies." I laughed to myself as I thought about how earnest his face had been when he'd tried to sell me that line. "Maybe Archer was too."

"I mean, you could mow down dozens of them with this thing." She picked up an automatic rifle I doubted was even legal, then put it back with a weird look on her face. "I'd rather hit someone. Seems more satisfying."

I could see it. Dylan was curvy and feminine, but I had little doubt she could kick some ass if need be.

"It's fucking Christmas." Merc whistled low and walked into the room, Cam on his heel with two large duffle bags.

Merc went right for the rifle his sister had just held, pointed it at the ground, and unloaded it with several quick, well-practiced hand motions. "Cam, brother—"

"There are more." Cam tossed the bags on the bed and picked up several boxes of ammo and shoved them in.

He glanced up at me with a sexy half grin. "The other night, I thought I was a dead man when I heard you in here. Figured someone had found Archer's stash. Scared the shit out of me."

"I'm betting I was more afraid than you." I stepped toward the door, making room for the boys and their toys. There were four long guns, a shorter barreled shotgun, and almost a dozen pistols. I had a hard time imagining the need for that many.

Merc took apart and unloaded the rifles before stashing them in the other bag.

"Nobody in this room is going to hurt you, darlin." Cam watched me across the bed, a box of bullets in his hand. "But it goes without saying, for all of us—nobody ever hears about this."

"I got you." Merc nodded and went back to work.

"Leave the thirty-eight, that chrome forty-five, and a rifle." He spoke first to Merc, but his eyes never left mine. "We good?"

Asking me to keep his secrets required a massive amount of trust. I was proud he put that much in me. But the resounding drum beat in my head reminded me that this was a world I didn't belong in. My mouth opened and a single word came out. "Absolutely."

"You think it's that bad?" Dylan whispered.

Merc sent her a glance that told her to mind her own business, but she didn't back down. "I have a right to know."

This was obviously a familiar argument, because Merc sighed heavily.

"But you don't." His voice was calm, but underneath there was an edge.

I backed fully into the hallway, just outside the door. Family squabbles were not something I wanted to be in the middle of.

"He's right." Cam zipped up the bag filled with guns and set it on the floor. "Club business isn't yours."

"This is more than that and you know it." She held her ground, arms crossed, and her chin thrust out in defiance.

Cam's loaded gaze flicked from me to her, and he didn't need to say more. Dylan stalked out of the room and down the hallway, forcing me back in when all I wanted to do was be somewhere else.

"Grab the bags and put them in the truck. We can come back for the rest of the shit later."

Merc snorted. "Another felony won't fucking matter."

But he took off with both duffels, leaving Cam and me alone in Archer's bedroom, surrounded by what was left of a life I couldn't understand.

He seemed to struggle with a lot of things in the quiet that stretched out between us. I went into the closet and pulled boxes from the top shelf—something I'd been doing before Dylan and I'd started finding rifles.

The space was a walk-in, but small and cramped. When Cam filled the doorway, I should have felt trapped. I didn't. Instead, I turned back to him, a flush heating my chest. "You don't owe me an explanation. Hopefully, I won't be here long enough to get in your way."

"It's not that." His face held a somber expression, his tone serious, leaving the entire closet chilled. "I need you to be careful. You went to the store the other day, and that's cool, but don't go anywhere without letting me know."

His words cooled whatever warmth being close to him had given me. He certainly didn't have to tell me things. I had no right to question him, but the longer I stayed, the more I wanted to. The chill grew until I half expected to see my breath when I spoke. "What happened to Archer?" My father. Why would any man need an entire freaking arsenal in his bedroom?

Without answering, Cam walked away. "I'll be back later. Dylan will stick around most of the day. Text if you find anything else," he called over his shoulder.

I didn't relax until I was alone. It wasn't Cam that was scary. He was strong, sexy, and a slew of things I shouldn't even think about. But whatever was happening beneath the surface here was something much bigger.

The closet smelled of him even after he left the room. I inhaled the scent. Leather from his vest, and a clean masculine smell that made me lick my lips.

There were three top shelves I'd cleared of boxes by the time Dylan came back. "Who knew Archer would have a thing for reading westerns?" She rifled through a box of books.

"And political thrillers." I dropped another box with a thud beside her.

"That does *not* surprise me." She chuckled.

As she knelt by the boxes, she looked up at me and pursed her lips in contemplation. "Desert Kings' business stays with the MC, even if half my family wears the patch. Wives, daughters, sisters, old ladies... we get stonewalled until they need something. Like I told you, we can't ask questions."

The frustration was evident as she turned back to the box and pushed books around. "It pisses me off, because I could help if they'd let me."

"Cam tell you anything?" She didn't look up, just drug a finger down the broken spine of a well-worn volume.

"No." I sat on the edge of the bed and pulled my knees to my chin. "But he's only known me a week. Why would he?"

She shrugged. "Who knows? You're Archer's kid—"

"He hasn't even told me how he died."

This time, Dylan's eyes were stormy as she sat back on the floor and leaned against the wall in front of me. "They found him in a motel room in town, a single gunshot wound to his head. Gun in his hand."

Whatever I'd thought, it hadn't been that he'd killed himself. I gripped myself tight and rested my chin on my knees.

"Cam doesn't believe he killed himself. I don't think my dad does either."

Which explained the secrecy. We both sat together as the sun set and turned the blinds from a blinding white to a glowing orange. When I couldn't take it any longer, when more questions than I had a right to ask tumbled around in my head, I went back to the closet and fished out old ball caps and motorcycle magazines.

"Find anything?" she asked me later.

"Maybe." My fingers brushed across a well-cared for, glossy wooden box and pulled it from the back of the top shelf.

When I opened it, all the air in the room got sucked away. There were hundreds of pictures of me, the one on top was from my high-school graduation. At the bottom, a large manilla envelope. I placed the box on the dresser and shook out the letters.

My heart ached. The careful, flowing cursive was as familiar to me as my own handwriting.

Mom.

He'd known. Every milestone, every part of my life, she'd written to him. I lowered myself to the ground and started reading.

"I think you found it."

"Huh?" I flicked a glance up at her.

"Whatever you were looking for." She hugged me before disappearing out of the room to leave me alone with the letters.

Maybe it wasn't Archer I'd needed, but Mom. I moved the box to the spare room and sat on the bed, reading through her letters, looking at the pictures. I'd always felt her love, but she had never been an emotional person. Closed off, guarded, sometimes cold. But reading her words, I could feel the love she'd never been able to express.

I lay on the bed at one point, clutching a letter to my chest.

It was dark by the time I heard the truck come back and both bikes leave. Dylan called her goodbyes not long after.

Archer had kept up with every aspect of my life the whole time. There were printed emails too, from teachers and coaches, people who'd been in my life through the years. And yet, I'd never known a thing about him. She'd told me he was a dangerous, horrible man. Made it such a big deal I never tried to seek him out myself.

There was even a copy of my graduation invitation Mom had mailed to him. He hadn't come, but from the looks of an email, she had thanked him for sending money. How hypocritical to say such awful things but then take from him.

The box did little to heal me. Instead, I fell asleep thinking of all the things I'd missed out on.

It was after three a.m. when the sound of Cam's bike roared up the driveway and woke me. How it must hurt to know that someone you cared so much for, looked up to, had taken their own life.

Could his disbelief be denial? I didn't know, but my heart still ached for Mom. Even if she'd lied to me my entire life. Losing someone you loved changed who you were. Not knowing why, the surprise of it coming so fast, then having that death thrown up in your face when his estranged daughter comes to town?

The more he softened around me, the more that guard dropped, the more I realized I liked him. Yeah, he was sexier than any guy I'd ever met, and dangerous too. But he was funny, kind and loyal. He hadn't done anything to me, not really.

But the way his lips curved up under the blond goatee when he grinned at me, or the way his voice got lower when we were alone...

I twitched uncomfortably on the bed, jerking the Harley Davidson throw blanket up to my chin. Thinking about Cam definitely wouldn't lull me back to sleep.

Stretching as I stood, I packed up the wooden box and stowed it beneath my suitcase. When I left here, these things were coming with me. Everything else could stay.

If I was awake, I might as well get to work. I started a pot of coffee. Outside, the lights were on in Cam's over the garage apartment. He was awake too. I snarled at my reflection in the dark glass when the thought tightened my belly.

I moved my clothes around in the laundry and deposited clean ones in the guest room. The mundane chore, surrounded by the familiar and comforting scent of detergent and fabric softener, made me feel momentarily at home.

That feeling clawed its way from my chest and up my throat. I didn't have a home. In a few weeks, when this was over, I'd have money but nowhere to belong.

I steadied myself when I reached to pick up an errant sock off the kitchen floor. Archer's vest still hung on the back of the chair. They'd given it to me, but it wasn't mine. Even if I'd known him, I wasn't part of that world.

But Cam was. The surrogate son. It belonged to him.

Clad only in a pair of shorts that flirted with the hem of my faded t-shirt, I snatched it off the chair and took off out the back door. Cam was up. I could give it to him now. Maybe offer him some sort of closure, peace, something...

At the top of the steps, I faltered. Low music hummed through the walls, followed by laughter, and a woman's voice purring.

Nope. Nope. Nope.

This was a horrible idea. I don't know what made me think a guy like Cam Savage would be up this late alone. I turned and jogged down the wooden stairs, thankful my bare feet made little noise.

The music grew louder as his door swung open.

I froze halfway down the steps. There were cameras. I forgot about the cameras. *Shit.*

"Riley?" His voice was sultry, sleepy.

I died on the spot, my legs weak and my stomach heavy.

"Um, yeah, it's nothing." I clung to the vest and jogged down a few more.

"Wait a damn minute." The wood of the deck groaned a little as he walked out.

But I wasn't stopping. "No, it's cool. No big deal. I'll talk to you about it tomorrow."

"Darlin, *stop*." His exasperated demand rolled through me like a thunderclap.

I stopped and turned, clutching Archer's vest to my chest.

Cam was already coming down the stairs, shirtless, in a pair of jeans, his hair tousled. It was unfair that he looked that good, even right now. Or maybe what he'd been up to had been the reason he looked so soft and sexy.

Damn. My cheeks heated and my tongue got thick. I was an idiot. I thrust the leather at him when he was only a few steps above me.

With a confused look, he examined Archer's cut.

"It's yours, not mine. I was thinking about it and... yeah. This should have never been given to me. Anyway, have a good night." I spun and tried not to speed walk like the elderly at the mall.

"For fucks' sake." He wrapped his long fingers around my elbow and jerked me to a stop on the concrete.

When I turned, his face was set in an almost painfully earnest expression, which somehow made the entire situation more embarrassing. Especially when a bleached blond with more fake lashes than good sense leaned over the rail.

"You coming back, Cam baby? I wasn't done yet." She giggled and gave me a mean snarl behind his back.

"Nah, we're done, Krystal. You can go." He watched me, studying me with such intensity I wiggled free from his grasp and tugged on the hem of my shirt. The childhood nervous habit coming back with such ferocity, I wanted to puke.

I couldn't figure out if he was waiting for her to leave before he said anything to me or if he wanted my reaction to her. Which embarrassed me more.

I gave him nothing. Mostly because I felt like a fish washed up on the beach. Every part of me was itchy, and I was floundering internally.

"Are you fucking kidding me?" She rounded the corner of the railing, looking like she was about to explode. She'd turned red, even the cleavage her push-up bra was tossing over the neckline of her shirt.

"No." He glanced back at her and jerked his chin toward the driveway. "Kick rocks."

My gasp of shock was quickly swallowed by a laugh I covered with my hand. She glared down at me before stomping back inside.

"I'm going inside." I tried to pull away, but he held fast to my arm.

"Please don't." He loosened his grip until it wasn't tight, but warm. If I'd really tried to pull free, he would have released me. I wasn't sure I wanted to, so I didn't. And the please had probably cost him more than he would admit.

Krystal wasn't the only woman to exit his apartment. Another one, looking far more sheepish with her arms full of clothes and her bag, followed with her head down. Krystal, though, was fuming and practically hissed at me as she stormed by us.

"Two of them?" I coughed out before I could stop myself. "Wow."

As they disappeared around the house, one side of his upper lip curled up and he gave a mischievous lift of his brow.

I was absolutely out of my league with this guy.

"Hot, right?" He was still grinning.

"Excessive," I responded, deadpan.

The momentary apprehension on his face was new, and I relished it with a disinterested shrug. Waiting on Krystal and her friend to leave had given me time to find stable ground and steady myself.

He frowned, glanced down at the vest in his hand, and opened his mouth, but no sound came out. When he looked back at me, I was reminded of what made walking up those steps so nerve-wracking. He wasn't just attractive. Every part of him appealed to me on a level I'd never experienced. There wasn't a man anywhere that had heated me right down to the soles of my feet like one look from Cam Savage could.

"Wanna go for a ride?"

And just like that, he sent me topsy-turvy all over again.

Ten

CAM

Bringing Krystal and her friend home with me had been the biggest act of self-sabotage I'd executed in a year or more. Shaking Krystal would have been impossible if I'd followed through. I should thank Riley for the interruption.

Every notification from the camera drew my attention, even with Krystal and her friend trying their best to distract me.

Letting Riley walk away down those steps had been impossible.

Hell, even two chicks hadn't stopped me from thinking of her. I'd been good before, but fuck...this was hard. There'd been women I desired that I didn't fuck. I could stop thinking of them, bang someone else, and soothe the itch.

This was different. *She* was different. The look on her face when I'd asked her to go for a ride was unexpected and hit me like knuckles to the gut. Instantaneous excitement and pleasure. I knew the feeling well. But damn, when it came from her, it left me half hard. Which was more than Krystal had managed with her mouth all over me.

And then there was Archer's cut.

I laid it lovingly across my small kitchen table, folded to show his well-earned center patch. I had to fight back the emotion as I yanked a clean shirt out and jerked it over my head, then shouldered into my own.

"Never ride without it." The ghost of Archer's words the day he'd handed me my first cut echoed in the small apartment. *"It's more than leather, Prospect."*

I'd lived the life every day since and never questioned it. Not even when he'd had me ride with him to keep tabs on his kid.

She'd always been pretty, smart, everything I couldn't have. I'd known it then, but attraction was easy to ignore from a distance.

Not when she was right in front of me.

I grabbed a Kings hoodie and jogged down the steps. She stood under the carport. I braced myself to see her. I moved with the stab of lust that rocketed from my chest to my crotch instead of having it stop me short.

This was Archer's kid he'd fought so hard to protect, to shield from the world we lived in—the one he'd created. Here I was, pulling her further into it.

But would he have wanted me to shuffle her along, homeless and alone?

No.

She wore long sleeves, but when I held the hoodie to her, she smiled with relief. "All my cool weather stuff is in storage." She pulled it over her head.

I bit my lip. She looked fuck-all delicious in something that I'd worn, that I knew smelled like me, with the Club's insignia all over it.

I could march her up the stairs and not leave for a full ass week.

Instead, I behaved. Or as well as I could as I popped the lid onto her head, strapped it under her chin, and grabbed her a pair of safety glasses.

She looked at the clear plastic glasses like I'd given her a handful of worms.

"More bugs at night, sweetheart. Attracted to the light. I'd keep your mouth shut, too."

Or not. The thought of that sent a rush of blood to my balls.

Her smile was amused and warm. The sort of thing that should put a man at ease. Instead, it felt so intimate that it twisted my gut around.

I climbed on first and watched over my shoulder as she got on. "My bike is a different animal from Archer's. You need to hang on tight..." I gestured around my waist as I explained. "...especially when I get on it, or you'll come off."

Not that I'd ever thrown anyone off my bike. Maybe I just wanted her close.

She eyed me dubiously and scooted closer as I fired it up. Her body was warm, her touch tentative as she wrapped her arms around my middle.

I idled out of the driveway, careful not to rev the engine too much until we throttled out of the neighborhood. At the last stop sign, I grabbed her hands and tugged her arms tighter around me—forcing her even closer. My palms lingered on her soft skin, the warmth of it drawing my attention, and the rest of my body reacted.

If she'd dropped her hands, I'd have embarrassed myself.

I cautioned a glance at her through my mirror.

"You ready?" I shouted over the throttle pop and watched her eyes light up in anticipation.

But it was the way her tongue darted out between her lips that sent me roaring off into the night. I grinned when I hit second gear hot and she squeezed so hard it felt as though she might crawl into my cut with me.

Archer's place was near two separate highways. We were out of Dry Valley in less than ten minutes. I didn't relax until I was hitting eighty and the city lights faded behind me. The more distance I put between us and my problems, the more like myself I felt.

I slowed when we crossed the county line. My reach out here if I got pulled over would only go so far without calling Preacher or AP. I damn sure didn't want Preacher to know I was out like this, riding with Riley.

He didn't need to know shit about her.

The defiant protective streak shot through me like a forty-five, ripping at ideals that had been all but pounded into every fiber of my being. No woman before the club. Brotherhood above all else.

I'd only known her a week. The reaction was stupid. I put a few miles of deserted interstate between myself and that feeling. Archer would expect me to protect Riley and I would. The quicker I could get her out of here, the easier all our lives would be.

She shifted behind me, laying her helmet against the back of my shoulder. We'd been riding for a while and were in familiar territory, so I took the next exit and headed toward a diner that meant something to me and might mean something to her.

I recognized the little red sedan parked out back and couldn't help the little niggle of pleasure. Sometimes—like Archer's funeral—official club shit got in the way of things. Like spending time with the people who came that were important to me.

Riley didn't need my help to crawl off the bike when I parked, and she was smirking when I moved to help her with her helmet.

"Hang on? You didn't tell me riding with you would be like having my stomach sucked out through my throat. It definitely didn't feel like that during the funeral." Her hazel eyes twinkled with flecks of green and gold like the river over rocks after a rain.

Everything here was so dry and barren in the urge to dive in jarred me.

Fuck. This bitch made me poetic.

I laughed anyway, enjoying the happiness riding with her made her feel. My knuckles brushed against her throat as I popped the snaps and dropped the helmet on the seat.

"She's fast."

"I hope you mean the bike." She tossed me a snark-filled side eye that made me want to kiss it off her. "Because I saw what you sent packing, and I don't have the gear-ratio for that."

I laughed again. Who was this woman? "Where the—"

"Archer has all these bike magazines everywhere; I've been reading them." She blushed a little and looked away. "It helps since you guys speak such a different language."

She wanted to know. It was cute. And more, she was still talking about me kicking out Krystal and the other chick. Man, the things I could tell Riley—but she might hate me.

Could be a good thing.

I smiled to myself and held the door to the diner open. No one else was around—too early yet for the working people and too late for the drunks.

"Boy, you're the best-looking thing I've seen all day." A chirpy woman's voice blurted out across the empty restaurant.

The tall, skinny woman with dyed red hair and dark eye shadow wrapped me in a hug that took me back to the only good memories I had of being a kid.

"Ro." I squeezed her tight. She wasn't as frail as she had been last time. "It's good to see you."

"I wish you saw me more," she choked out but didn't cry. "Who's this?"

I pulled from her embrace to introduce them. "Riley, this stunning woman is Robbie. Ro, this is Riley Bowman." I gave her a minute for that to sink in. "Ro was my mom's best friend back in the day. Helped raise me and introduced me to Archer."

Robbie rolled her eyes. "I never should have."

I could tell by the way she kept glancing at Riley and the emotion in her voice, I'd made the right decision coming here.

"It worked out." I gave her a look. This argument was old, she never won, and things were better this way. There hadn't been many other options.

"Well, nice to meet you, Riley. Hungry? What do you like? I can have Sam make anything...take a look at the menu. Breakfast and dinner served all day." She seated us and turned back to me. "Coffee?"

"Yes, ma'am." I told her.

"What to drink, hon?" She looked at Riley.

Riley rattled off a soda and when she glanced back down to the menu, Ro's glance darted from my bike to my guest and her brow lifted in question. I shook my head no and checked the menu myself. Another argument I wasn't going to have.

Ro was well versed in the rules of the MC. Riding with Riley on the back of my bike meant I was staking a claim to her.

"My mom was a junkie." I spoke without looking up. "She and Ro went to school together. Ro never had any kids, so I was her fill-in."

Riley caught my gaze and pursed her lips with an annoyed tsk. "You're nobody's fill-in."

I shrugged. "You know what I mean. She got to take me to do the fun things, like buy me school clothes, carnivals, shit like that. When I was in middle school, my mom had a revolving door of new guys—some of them more violent than others. I stayed with Ro a lot back then." There was something about Riley that made me keep talking, no matter how many times I tried to shut up.

I'd never told anyone this shit. Some of this I doubted even Merc or Dylan would know.

"Figure out what you want?" Ro set down the coffee and Riley's soda.

"Pancakes." I grinned. I'd never eaten anything else here.

"With bacon, extra crispy." She finished with a coral-colored grin before looking at Riley.

"I'll do the same." She snapped the menu shut and spoke in a mock whisper to Ro. "Do we tell him I was going to order that anyway, or let him keep thinking he did something special?"

Ro seemed to contemplate it. "Eh, he's too cute. We let him think whatever he wants." Then she grinned and walked away.

"Why do I feel like you're both making fun of me?"

With a solemn, beautiful face, Riley grinned. "Aw, isn't he cute?"

I tossed a sugar packet at her and was rewarded with a bright smile as she snatched the little white packet from the air and laughed. I was so caught up in her beauty, I didn't dodge it when a quick flick of her wrist sent the packet smacking against the side of my face.

She could make fun of me for that too and I wouldn't care.

Eleven

Riley

This side of Cam was unexpected and surprising in the best kind of way. Sitting there, stretched out in a booth at a diner off the interstate, he was more relaxed than I'd ever seen him. His grin came easy, and he made jokes.

But the love he showed for the older woman, Robbie, spoke to my heart.

There were layers to Cam Savage, and I couldn't help myself from poking at them and peeling them back little by little.

"Thank you," I said, before sipping my soda through the straw.

Cam stretched one arm across the back of the booth and grinned at me over the rim of his coffee cup. "For what?"

"Not judging the ramblings of a drunk woman the other night. For not telling anyone. For being kind. I don't know, for everything."

"You don't owe me any gratitude. You don't owe anyone here shit." After several swallows, he put the cup down.

"Just because you don't think you deserve it, doesn't make it...*less*."

The way he watched me was like he was finding a place to put my words. He heard them, he understood them, but he wasn't quite sure what he was supposed to do with them.

I kind of felt that way anytime I talked to anyone.

"Being alone sucks." He spun the half-empty cup, his tone contemplative and a little sad. "Having no one to lean on, nowhere to belong, is the worst feeling in the world."

A part of my chest felt like it was being jerked through my skin. My breaths were suddenly painful. I looked out the window into the empty parking lot to keep from looking at him, so he couldn't see me flinch.

He was right, but I didn't need a reminder that in a week I'd be right back where I was. A little cushion for my landing but flying solo. The lone streetlight blinked every few seconds, threatening to go out. That's how it felt to be me. The bright spots were brief and constantly interrupted by the darkness.

"Is that why you joined the club?"

"Patched in." He was still studying me, like he was afraid he'd spook me. "You have to be invited. Archer—" he tilted his head toward Robbie "—dated Ro for a while, sponsored me."

I blinked once. He'd brought me here, not to show me a side of himself but to show me something about Archer only he could.

"She knew your mom, too."

The way he said that stopped me. He'd said only a few Desert Kings had known I existed. He was obviously one of them. I couldn't process Ro, or what she knew about my parents. Not yet.

"How long did you know about me?" I absently twirled the straw around the large cup.

"A while." He didn't sip the coffee. Instead, he spun the cup on the table, mirroring my motions with the straw, and watched me. It was like he was deciding what to tell me.

"I moved in with him when I was about sixteen. Shit with my mom got too deep, she OD'd, and I was too much for Ro to handle. I think he told me about you as a way to relate. We're close to the same age."

"But he didn't even know me."

Cam shrugged, then leaned across the table. "Even if he hadn't, darlin, I'm pretty sure he wouldn't have wanted you riding around with me in the middle of the night."

There was a sexy rumble to his voice, but I snorted a laugh. "I'm so scared."

"Maybe you should be." It wasn't his words, but the way he narrowed his eyes, like a predator zeroing in on his dinner.

I shivered. "Archer keep you out of trouble?"

"Got him *in* way more than out." Robbie snorted a half laugh as she expertly passed plates from her arm to the table.

"I'm going to wash my hands." Cam slipped out of the booth.

Robbie busied herself at the table arranging a fresh bottle of syrup until he was out of earshot.

"He's never brought a woman to see me." Ro sighed. "I was excited for a minute until he told me who you were."

I flinched and my stomach tightened.

Reading my expression, she hurried on. "Oh no, nothing bad, honey. I'm sorry I phrased it like that. Archer's kid? Of course, he'd keep you close. Your daddy would want him to, that's all I meant."

"And you knew him well, my...dad?"

She sat in Cam's seat. "I did. Your mom too. I didn't get with him until after she'd left, but we were all close at one point."

I had so many questions, but I was lost. Anything I'd want to ask would take time to unpack and the answers even longer.

She stared toward where the restroom door swung shut. "Cam's got a good heart. Life hasn't been kind to him, but he keeps dusting himself off." She turned her gentle eyes toward me. "Life's been a dick to you too, huh?"

I laughed. "Yeah."

"I should have never introduced him to the Kings. But—the shit he got into wasn't going away. Not without help."

It's like she wanted me to ask her so she could relieve her burden. But it wasn't my place, so I didn't. She changed it up. "Don't trust any of them, except Cam. For what your daddy did for him, he'd step in front of a train for you, girl. If you want to talk about your daddy or anything else, give me a call. Cam has my number."

I didn't quite know what to do with that. She stood and met him halfway back to the table for another hug. The sun was rising, and other customers trickled in.

Disappointment made the food in front of me less appealing. A part of me had hoped that his attention was something other than a misplaced sense of duty. Robbie had confirmed the truth.

With a sigh, I poured a swirling trickle of syrup onto my pancakes as Cam sat back down.

"These are the best." He took the syrup and dumped a heaping amount on his stack before digging in. He ate several bites before looking up. "Eat."

Making a face, I plucked a piece of bacon off my plate and took a bite. What should have been a salty, savory experience tasted hard and dry. "I am."

He shook his head. "You don't want me crawling over there and feeding you. We'd make a scene." A mischievous spark lit his eyes and his lips twisted into a devilish grin.

Was he flirting with me? I narrowed my gaze, stabbed a bite of pancake, and shoved too much in my mouth. Without another word, I ate dutifully and quietly for several minutes, each bite feeling like cement in my stomach.

Finally, he pushed his mostly empty plate to the center of the table, leaned forward on his elbows, and steepled his fingers under his chin. "What did I miss?"

I flicked one eyebrow up and chewed my last piece of bacon.

"Did Ro say something to upset you?" He leaned back like he was about to leave the table.

"No." I wiped my mouth and waved my napkin like a white flag between us. "So hard to believe I wouldn't be all excited at the prospect of you feeding me something?"

He frowned. "That's not what I mean." His words were measured and made me irrationally angry.

I knew I shouldn't be mad at him. He hadn't led me on. In fact, all he'd been was nice and an occasional flirt. Guys like Cam Savage expected women to melt at their feet. But it was easier to be mad at him than myself, for somehow imagining something between us.

"Why two?" I asked, cooly, changing the subject to something that I had the high ground on.

"Huh?" He was genuinely confused for several seconds. Then realization settled on his face, and he rubbed his lips together. "Okay, let's do this. But outside."

He pulled cash from his hip pocket, far more than necessary to cover the meal, and tossed the bills on the table.

I followed him out, letting my anger grow until the warmth spread out down my arms and I had to push up the sleeves of his hoodie. I gritted my teeth to keep from jerking it off and tossing it at him.

Cam stopped at his bike, leaned back on the seat, pulled a pack of cigarettes out of his pocket, and lit one. "This is where you're going to go all raging feminist on me, right?"

"I don't even know what that means. I just want to know why. Why two women not one? Is one not good enough? Didn't the one deserve better or are you naturally a pervert?"

I should have had this conversation before the ride, but...the idea of the ride had been almost all-consuming. And then there was Cam. He turned me into someone I wasn't.

"And now I've got at least one groupie that hates me for interrupting what-ever you were doing. She probably wants to claw my eyes out, and I'm definitely not doing any of what she was doing—with you."

"One would have been just fine, darlin. You offering?" There was a challenge on his smug face that made me want to ball up my fists and scream.

Mostly because if he offered, I'd say yes. It wasn't Cam I was angry with, but myself. Angry, confused, scared and a host of other things.

"You only answered one question." I did, at least, make fists. I stopped just before I settled them on my hips like an irate teenager.

He took another drag, pinched the cigarette between his thumb and fore-finger like a joint, thumped the ashes, and contemplated the glowing tip with a mocking smile. "Darlin, I've got a feeling telling you it was her idea is going to really piss you off."

"No more than treating them both like dirt on the bottom of your shoe." I tried not to growl at him. The urge to do so was so foreign to me, I shifted my weight from foot to foot and searched for something that felt like myself. "You told her to kick rocks."

His laugh rang out across the parking lot, drawing an older couple's attention as the husband held the car door open for his wife. They probably thought we were on drugs.

He probably was.

"You would rather I went back up?" He stood from the bike and blew out smoke before he tossed the cigarette out into the parking lot. "Shut that door and let one go down on me while I made out with the other one?"

I held a hand up and flinched. "Stop."

"I answered your question; you answer mine."

I swallowed the spiny ball of misplaced jealousy and closed my eyes. "No." My voice wavered far more than I wanted it to.

When I opened them, he was right there. I had a brief second to register the heat of his breath against my face before he kissed me.

His lips on mine were like having all the air sucked out of a room. There was a tickle in my stomach, and I couldn't get enough.

He tasted of tobacco and menthol, of coffee and something sexier, darker. His tongue was wicked as it pushed past my lips and plundered. His facial hair was short enough to tickle, brushing across my lips as he sucked my tongue into his mouth, raked his teeth over it.

I gripped the sides of his vest, the well-worn leather softer than I expected. His calloused, long-fingered hand slipped across my jaw and against my neck, before cupping the back of my head to gently guide me.

The movement tilted my chin up, gave him more access, and all at once I was scalding hot but trembling like it was freezing. I pressed my body to his, practically climbing him, and rubbed my tongue against his, losing myself in the pure pleasure of the kiss.

He left me dizzy when he pulled away, dropping his hand so that he absently brushed both my arms.

"That better, princess?" he asked, his voice airy and breathless in a way that stoked a fire at my core.

No, it wasn't better. Absolutely nothing made sense. Two weeks ago, I was sleeping in my car, fending off greasy truckers, and wondering if I'd be able to eat the next day. Now I stood, shaking, having just had my mind blown by possibly the sexiest man I'd ever seen.

Who the hell was I?

"I hate you." I dropped my forehead to his shoulder and, still holding his vest, made a fist and nudged him gently in the side.

He oofed and hugged me to him. "No, you don't."

I didn't, but I wanted to. What little I knew about him, the good outweighed the bad. Every new thing made him more attractive. I wasn't angry that he'd brought two girls home the night before. He was right there, too; I'd wished it was me.

He let me go and grabbed the helmet. "We need to go. I'm beat."

I stopped thinking about myself and really looked at him. His eyes were bloodshot and while his lips were still swollen from our kiss, there were dark circles forming under his eyes and lines around his mouth.

"Can you ride back?"

He dropped a kiss on my forehead before putting the helmet on. "Awe, isn't she cute?"

I snatched the straps from him and hooked them myself. "Sunrise first kisses are supposed to be more romantic."

He threw a long leg over the bike and cranked it before shouting at me. "It was hot, though."

Yeah, it totally was.

The evening news had called for a warmup from the unseasonably cool desert weather. And even on the bike, with the wind whipping around me, I felt the temperature rise on the way home. Could have been Cam, too. Pressing against him after that kiss definitely hadn't cooled me off.

This time the ride felt more precarious as Cam wove in and out of morning traffic. It wasn't the fast roar of the engine, empty highway ride that exploded through me like a bolt of lightning. I didn't flinch, but I was keenly aware of how close every car or truck got.

Worse, the rush of air from passing eighteen wheelers felt like it might push us off the road.

Cam didn't seem to notice.

I didn't relax until he took the exit into town and slowed. There was less traffic here. What trickled out did so in the opposite lane—morning commuters heading to Vegas for work or to gamble, you never could tell in this desert.

By the time we turned onto Archer's street, I was comfortable enough to rest my hands on my knees. Until Cam shot up the angled driveway, jarring me in my seat enough that I grabbed his waist again and clung tight.

He grinned at me in the side mirror, making it obvious he'd done it on purpose.

Under the carport, with the roar of the motor reverberating all around us, I hopped off the bike. Touching him was a reminder of the kiss, which warmed me in places I'd never considered. My physical reaction to Cam Savage was shiny, new, and bothersome.

I pulled the hoodie over my head and handed it to him as he shut down the engine. Was it the heavy garment that made me sweat or my proximity to him?

Putting distance between us was the best plan. I needed to shower before Dylan came over, anyway.

Cam grabbed my hand before I could take a full step away from him.

"Riley, come here." His voice was cool, firm, and crashed into me like a bucket of cold water.

Something was wrong.

Twelve

CAM

Cam

The back door stood open, splinters of glass littered doorway, and the wood was cracked. Everything around me slowed down, and I slipped the nine-millimeter out of my saddlebag and chambered a round.

I pulled out my phone and shot off a text.

Archer's. 911.

The entire table would be here within fifteen minutes, maybe less. But I wasn't standing out here like a sitting duck. The entire neighborhood had heard me roll in.

"Stay behind me." I shouldered my body in front of Riley and put her hand on my vest.

She took the hint and clung to the bottom edge.

Blood pounded in my ears as I pushed the door the rest of the way open with my knuckles. As quietly as I could, I stepped through the broken glass and took a two-hand grip on the pistol. If someone was in there, I'd shoot first and ask questions later.

The kitchen was clear, as was the small laundry room to the side. I swept across the living room—the couch had been tossed and the entertainment center doors were open. But no one was there hiding in the corners.

Taking the narrow hallway made me nervous. All the bedrooms and main bathroom branched off it. I couldn't explore one without leaving another empty.

I'd done this once already this week, only that time it had been different. Then, I'd been alone. Stopping at the end of the hall, I took a deep breath and glanced to my left. A figure filled the doorway we'd just come in.

Puck's eyes held mine, and he pulled a gun from the small of his back. I'd not heard him ride up and he didn't have on his cut. He'd driven something else.

I pushed Riley at him and jerked my head toward the backyard. She glanced at me, confused. Puck understood, waving her over and ushering her out the back door. He'd take care of her. I had to trust that.

A cold sweat broke out across my skin, the edges of my vision clouded, and the pulse thundering in my ears was so loud I worried I wouldn't hear anyone come up behind me.

I checked Archer's small office first; it was trashed. Paper and folders littered the floor and the rolling chair was upended. I stifled a half grin—anything important had been on his laptop. Which wasn't in this house. I wasn't that stupid.

Across the hall, the guest room, the one Riley used, was untouched. I even checked the small bathroom and closet. Nothing. Archer's room, though, we'd interrupted whoever it was. As they'd only opened a few drawers, and the closet was already empty. A quick glance under the bed showed the remainder of his self-protection arsenal was still intact.

By the time I walked back out the back door, I was relaxing, but needed a smoke like nobody's business. I cleared my gun and stuck it in my belt before lighting a cigarette.

"Well?" Riley's eyes were wide, her face ashen.

The urge to pull her to me and hold her was strong. I ignored her question and looked past her to Puck, who leaned against a post on the carport, scratching his beard.

"Whoever broke in was looking for something. They took off out the back bathroom window. Screen's laying in the dirt." I took a drag, letting the nicotine soothe me.

Several Harleys popped and crackled up the driveway. Preacher and Jester, I'd heard the engines so many times I knew. Preacher's rumbled like an old dead hog, and Jester's had the hum of a racing engine beneath its crackle. They pulled into the carport and shut their bikes off in tandem, the sudden quiet eerie.

"The fuck happened?" Preacher was climbing off all fake concern. "You okay, sweetheart?" He went to Riley first. He reached for her face, and I straightened.

I'd kill him right here.

She took a step back and his hands fell to her shoulders like he would hug her if she needed to be consoled.

"I'm fine." She edged closer to me.

Preacher made a face, glaring at me before he continued, "What happened?"

"Cam and I rode to breakfast and when we came back..." She pointed to the door. "Looks like someone broke in, but Cam checked the house."

Oh, he heard that. Those first six words settled on the washed-up old fucker like a bundle of barbed wire. I couldn't help but grin at her. He wasn't the only one that heard it. There were rules, lines drawn in the sand, ones the table wouldn't even let Preacher break.

Riley Bowman was officially mine as far as the Kings were concerned. She was safe. At least, from one particular set of dangers.

"Somebody was looking for something. Fucked shit up in there pretty good." I finished my cigarette, dropped it on the concrete, and snubbed it out with my boot.

Jester lit a joint and passed it to me. "We calling the cops?"

Preacher looked at me with an expression that asked what I thought. Not that he cared, he'd do whatever he wanted. That he asked me—the VP—was for appearances only. Puck disappeared to the front of the house, moving quick for someone with that much sheer bulk.

I hit the joint and held the smoke for as long as I could before passing it back. Hell, my adrenaline was running so hot I could smoke the whole thing myself and probably wouldn't catch a buzz.

"I don't think it's going to do any good." It wasn't a lie. But the way Preacher was acting, the only part of this situation that seemed a surprise was Riley riding on the back of my bike. I didn't like that.

Riley sat at the table, quietly checking her phone as we talked.

"I'll take a look around." Preacher nodded to me once and ducked inside.

I didn't realize I'd stood so rigid in his presence until he walked away, and the muscles in my back relaxed. He'd been with Jester, so he couldn't have done it unless Jester had helped.

Nah, Jester isn't helping him do shit.

With the exception of a few punks like Ghost and Band Aid, Preacher hadn't built a very good connection with the younger guys. He wasn't a surrogate father like Archer had been or AP was.

Puck came back around. "They tried the front door first. Fucked the lock all up, I'm going to run and pick up a new windowpane and lock, get that fixed today. Shop is closed so I don't have to be there. Did you check the cameras?"

Fuck. I checked them then, but there was nothing after Riley and I left. "Cameras don't have shit, not even us pulling in."

"Let me see." Jester took my phone and fucked with it for a few minutes before Preacher came out. "Looks like someone fried the Wi-Fi on them. We'll need to check the modem, but I'll probably have to get new cameras. This time I'll do a dedicated system, so it's hard wired in and they can't fry them."

"So, there are no cameras?" Riley was getting freaked out now. Her eyes darting from me to Jester to Puck and back again, her face increasingly pale.

If I went to her, held her, that said more than I needed it to—*fuck.*

I swore and raked my fingers through my hair before hitting the joint again. When I offered it to her, she thought about it for a long second before shaking her head no. Hell, it would do her some good right about now.

"We won't let anything happen to you, Riley." Preacher jogged down the steps, his t-shirt clad beer belly jostling as he did. "You can come down to the clubhouse and hang out. We'll be there all day."

The rest of the patched officers rode up the driveway, climbed off bikes, and spilled into the carport.

The one to cut straight to me and survey the damage was Merc. "Damn."

I shrugged, and we said nothing. I knew he thought someone was after the guns. Good thing we'd cleared them out. Not that I agreed, but better safe than shot up.

"We got that run tomorrow, Cam. You good for it?" This from AP, who eyed me with the concern of a favorite uncle.

I nodded my head.

"I'll keep an eye on the kid while you do it." Preacher stepped in, once again trying to get Riley away from me. "We don't know who—"

"She can ride with me." I didn't wait for it, just dug my line in the sand deeper, filled it with gasoline, and set that bitch on fire.

Preacher balked, his ruddy face growing redder as he blustered without saying anything. He looked a damn fool. This young, beautiful woman had no interest in his old, perverted ass.

Fucking hell.

"It's a club thing, no women." He settled on, finally.

AP cut in. "We've done it before, he could use her as a smoke screen. See a problem with that, Jester?"

My Road Captain grinned. "I'm good with it. A little sad she ain't riding with me, though." He winked at me.

Riley's eyes had narrowed, but she ignored all of it. "Is it safe for me to go shower?"

"Your room's fine," I told her.

She was inside the house by the time my phone buzzed with a text from her. *Can I talk to you?*

I fired back. *Inside?*

Her. *Yes. Please.*

So formal. I almost grinned but hit the joint again when Jester passed it. Around me, they discussed the logistics of what had happened.

Need me to check under the bed? Or in it?

Her response was immediate. *I hate you.*

Thirteen

Riley

Riley

I regretted texting Cam as soon as I'd sent the last one. He wasn't my boyfriend. I had barely known him for a full week. The only person in this place I could trust, that was looking out for me was me.

Archer probably had some other angle, because lord knew he'd not helped me out when I needed it most. Now, I was being jerked around by a dead man. I was tired. I had a little money, but it wasn't enough to rebuild my life, which meant I had to stay until the will was read. But I couldn't wait it out in this house with all of them. Not after—I swallowed hard and wiped my clammy palms on my jeans.

"What's up?" Cam ducked into my room. His eyes were even more blood-shot, his golden lashes heavy on sleepy lids.

The effect was so incredibly sexy I had to focus on a chip in the paint over his shoulder just to form words that made sense. Why was he cuter now that I'd kissed him?

"I—so, I know y'all are going to need to be in and out of here today. Since there was a break in and..." *And none of you are calling the cops, like normal people would.* "... I'm going to rent a room for a few days."

In the short time I'd known him, I'd learned that he had one hell of a poker face. But he was tired, and I'd spent enough time studying him to see the subtle crinkle at the corners of his eyes and the tightness in his lips when he smiled.

"You don't need to do that." He fell onto my bed, folding his arms behind his head and stretching out one long leg. He kept the other on the ground.

The pillows would probably smell like him when I laid there later. The thought made me want to snuggle into them and wrap myself in his scent. I turned away and busied myself putting clean clothes back in my suitcase. "I'm not going to feel comfortable here."

"Go up to my place."

I shot him a *no way in hell* glance over my shoulder.

His throaty chuckle almost undid me and I gripped the side of my bag to keep from trembling with...what? Desire? Absolutely not. No way.

But...

"It was a kiss, princess. I'm not trying to climb into your panties." The room was quiet for a beat. "Unless you want me to."

"Oh, for the love of God." I smacked my suitcase shut and spun. "Can you be serious at all? I'm freaked and..." I fought with the vulnerability and sighed. "Preacher creeps me out."

The poker face cracked hard. His eyelids lowered so his eyes disappeared in the shadows of his lashes. "I'm worn the fuck out. You want a hotel, fine. Give me ten minutes to get some shit and I'll go with you. But I'm not leaving you alone."

When I stiffened, he sat up and shook his head, running his hands through his hair and speaking in low, almost inaudible syllables. "While you're here, I want you close. Because I don't trust him either."

Our gazes met, held, and I swallowed back the cold fingers of fear that crept up from my core. "Okay."

"I need a shower." He held his hands out, palms up. "No more flirting. Let's just crash. You can go up in a minute when I kick everyone out. Puck and Jester will be the only ones to come back. By then, you'll be upstairs."

What he didn't say was no one would think I was having sex with him. My reputation remained intact. Why'd he have to go and be honorable?

I followed Cam up the stairs, maintaining a safe distance, and busied myself looking anywhere but at him as he opened the door and held it for me. The last time we'd been on these stairs seemed like forever ago. I felt like a different person.

Had one kiss changed me that much?

His apartment was bisected into two main rooms. I stood in the first. The front half was the living area. In the back, an open doorway caught my gaze.

His room.

If Cam lounging on the bed I'd slept in made me feel all warm and breathy, glancing at his bedroom snatched the oxygen from my lungs.

"You can put your shit in there." He gestured to his room as he shrugged out of his cut and hung it on the back of a dark wood chair at a table in one corner. The pistol at his back flashed as his shirt lifted with the motion.

That was a startling reminder of why I was up here. The night before, two women had been in here doing—I didn't want to think of it, *or* deal with the jealousy that memory churned up.

"This is fine." I dropped my bag down on the overstuffed gray couch and crinkled my nose at his room.

He turned, leaned a hip on the table, and emptied his pockets. The brief glance he gave me glinted with amusement. "The bed is cleaner."

I made a face. "Excuse me?"

"You're thinking about last night. Trust me, darlin, you'll be the first woman in that room in a long time." He gave a half laugh and pointed at the couch. "Can't say that about the couch."

"Oh my God." I snatched up my bag and stomped to his room.

Crossing the threshold was like stepping into a different world. This was his place, a sanctuary. Dark blackout curtains held most of the Nevada sun at bay. What seeped in landed on pale walls with dark wooden floors. Each wall was adorned with at least one framed artistic shot of motorcycles or the desert.

One wall held a large flat screen television, and another two doors. One door stood open, revealing a tidy bathroom with a glass shower.

The bed was massive, with a dark wooden headboard. Surprisingly, this too was tidy. The black comforter was pulled tight, and the top edge folded back to reveal light pillows.

He stepped in behind me, so close his chest brushed against my back. The touch was almost non-existent, and my body responded as if he'd caressed me all the way down.

It was just a kiss, Riley. Damn.

On the far side of the bed was an upholstered chair. He took the small bag of clothes I'd brought up, put it on the chair, before he put his pistol and his phone on the modern, dark dresser trimmed in something metallic. Silver, maybe. "More pillows in the closet, if you want them."

The room was flooded with light from the bathroom as he stepped in and pulled off his shirt. I caught a glimpse of corded muscle and a tattoo across his shoulders before the door shut behind him.

His closet was as tidy as the rest of the room. I half expected to see his shirts organized by color, but they weren't. They hung to the right, his pants to the left. I pulled two pillows from a shelf and used them to make a barrier down the center of the bed.

I curled on the other half, listening as the water ran in the other room. Steam crawled under the door, bringing with it a tangy, citrus scent of a popular bar soap. One I'd held to my nose and inhaled as a kid. The smell soothed me then and did so now.

But I couldn't sleep. My entire body twitched and buzzed like every nerve was fighting against a weariness that sank me deeper into the mattress. Cam's bed was more comfortable than the one in Archer's guest room.

At least, that's what I told myself when I snuggled against his pillow and inhaled. The entire room smelled clean, almost sterile. Except the pillows. They smelled of Cam. Faint hint of woodsy tobacco, covered with something crisp and fresh—much like he'd tasted.

My stomach tightened, and my body broke out in a full-fledged hum that made it hard to shut my eyes. I might spend a few hours here, on Cam's bed, but I wasn't sleeping. Not like this.

I sat up, twisted so that my back popped and muscles relaxed. My entire life had been careful. I wasn't the sort of kid that ran down the steps headlong into the yard. I'd stayed with my hand on the rail, taking each stair carefully.

Life was a steady list of doing things I was supposed to, keeping my life as boring and safe as possible. Until Mom died. Every day since had been a struggle to survive. In only a few months I'd been so tired it hurt, so hungry I was sick, and so cold I couldn't stop shaking.

There were no friends to help pick me up off the ground. Those I'd had disappeared when Mom got sick—or maybe that had been my fault. I'd retreated, cared for her, felt sorry for myself.

Coming up here with Cam was out of character. I should have gone to a hotel. There was enough money. And yet...I *wanted* to make the bad decision. If only partially to be like the two women I'd interrupted him with.

The bathroom door opened before I'd laid back down. I could ignore him, and that he'd went in there without other clothes. Or...I could turn and...

I did and was rewarded with Cam in only a towel, wet hair tousled across his forehead. Beads of water traveled from the center point of his collarbone, down his chest, past his navel, to gather in the line of blond hair that disappeared beneath the towel slung low on his hips.

Damn.

Half gaping at him, I jerked my chin up and met his eyes. Heavy lidded again, the way they did when he knew exactly what I was thinking. He pushed his hair back from his face and winked before grabbing a pair of boxer briefs from the dresser.

He held my gaze in the dresser mirror for a split second. His slow sexual grin spoke to parts of me that really liked it.

I looked away, my face and chest hot, as he dropped the towel. There was only so much I could take. I wasn't prepared for that level of intimacy...not when I'd barely done more than make out with anyone.

And he had done so much more.

I dropped back to the bed with a huff, his chuckle teasing me. "Darlin, you keep it up and I'm going to test out this innocent act."

What was he talking about? My gaze narrowed as I caught his. Pretty blue eyes, bloodshot and half opened as he approached the bed. Something lingered there that would be demanding and take from me until I couldn't give anything else. Damn, how I wanted it to.

That feeling shocked me enough I swallowed any reply as he pulled the sheets down and climbed in. The way his muscles bunched and moved drew my gaze, made my body tense. Simple movements shouldn't be sexy. I looked away before I focused on the bulge at his groin.

I didn't look at him until the bed stilled. When I peaked, I was thankful I'd pulled a throw blanket over me. I don't think I could have handled being under the same sheet that covered his legs.

He lay sprawled on his back, much like he had on my bed. Only with one arm folded behind his head this time. The other was across his chest. Through the curtain of my lashes, I studied him.

Cam opened one eye and covered a yawn with the back of his hand. "Get some sleep, darlin."

"I will." And I pretended to for a while, before curiosity got the better of me.

His eyes were closed, his breathing steady and even, and with each rise of his bare chest, his body relaxed a little more. I didn't shut my eyes completely until he rolled against my pillow wall and tucked one against his chest, snoring ever so gently.

Only then did the buzzing in my muscles stop. The rumble of motorcycles shocked me from the verge of sleep once when Puck and Jester came back. After that, I slept and dreamed of what a man who kissed like Cam Savage could do with the rest of his body.

Fourteen

CAM

Cam

My entire life, my room was my sanctuary. The one place I wasn't looking over my shoulder for the knife coming at my back. In my room I could lock out the endless string of junkie boyfriends my mom brought through. When I was older, with Archer, my room was the place I could shrug out of the cut and the responsibilities it carried.

Caught in that brief, fuzzy place between sleep and wakefulness, I panicked. When I was a kid, I'd bolt upright, gasping and ready to fight. As an adult, I tempered that to a brief start—clenching my fists and waiting for the next bad thing to come at me. Even my sleep was a fight for survival.

But not this. The phone on my dresser bleeped an alarm. Two sharp tones and nothing more. This time, in that in between place, I burrowed into the inviting hum and stretched. My arm was heavy, pinned against something soft, pliant, warm.

Riley stretched against me, pressing into me so that her ass rubbed across my groin. I went from half mast, just waking up, to a raging hard on before she'd so much as mumbled in her sleep.

Damn.

Only a thin sheet separated us. I'd never woken up curled around a woman like this. Not even those I'd screwed. I'd never cared enough to stick around. *Or to leave yourself vulnerable.*

Choosing to ignore the voice in my head, I turned all my attention to Riley. In her sleep she'd rolled into me, the blanket she'd used thrown half over my legs. Her body was pliant against mine, teasing me. *Fuck.* I wanted her so bad.

I shouldn't.

I knew better.

But I nuzzled her head anyway, kissing the spot just behind her ear, then lower to the curve of her neck.

She stilled for a second, before she twined her fingers with mine and pulled my hand against her stomach. "Cam?"

Her tentative whisper barely audible over the hum of the air conditioner, but it was enough for me to pause. In that few seconds of quiet, I could vividly recall the way she'd tasted when I kissed her, the feel of her lips gliding across mine, and the way she'd surrendered to the pull between us. The careful, considerate young woman had turned into something else entirely. And I really liked being the one responsible.

I wanted more of it, needed it, *craved* it. But still, I waited.

"I've—I—" She stopped, unable to say more.

But I didn't need her to say it. I could see it. The innocence, the way she didn't seem to trust to look at me, the hesitant way she moved that was so fucking sexy.

Princess was a virgin.

The untouched thing was never a turn on, I preferred my partners willing and experienced. Time to bail. Abort Mission.

Not this time. Desire shot all the way from my chest to the tip of my cock that twitched with it. The first person to touch her, to be inside her, to make her come. *All Mine.*

I should leave. And yet... "Tell me when you want me to stop."

Nuzzling the hair from her neck with my nose, I kissed the skin there, nipping and suckling a line down her shoulder as I dragged my hand across her stomach and over her hip. I didn't stop the slide of my hand until her fingers slipped free.

Only then did I retrace the path, this time digging in a little with the blunt tips of my fingers.

Her little gasp told me I didn't have to be gentle. I shifted, letting her roll on her back beneath me. Hovering over her, much like that first night, I kissed her. She tasted of everything I'd ever needed. Warm, wet, and full of life. Her tongue twisted against mine, her fingers traced up my stomach, over my chest, and then down my arms, leaving little chills in their wake.

Even her touch drove me out of my mind.

When I broke the kiss, she reached for my face, confusion barely visible in the dim afternoon light from the living room.

I couldn't help but laugh. "Easy, darlin.'" I left her warmth long enough to kick out of the sheet and sweep the blanket away. With my knee between her thighs and a hand braced on either side of her head, I looked down, wishing I'd turned on the light. But I couldn't leave her, not even for a second.

"You're fucking beautiful." I said the words between ragged breaths.

She blushed and glanced away. The tiny hesitation was my undoing. She had no clue, absolutely none. Not of the men that turned to look when she walked in, of the way their gazes lingered, of how much I'd wanted her since that very first night when she'd fought against me.

She wasn't struggling now.

I dropped my head to her stomach, kissed the hem of the form hugging leggings she wore, and got the briefest taste of her skin there. Inhaling the heady scent of her, needing more, I pushed her shirt up and kissed the skin around her navel.

Riley's hips wiggled, and she squeaked a groan when I traced the rim of her belly button with the tip of my tongue.

"That...shouldn't be so hot," she gasped out.

Grinning against her, I kissed higher, alternating between kissing and sucking until my nose grazed her bra. I nipped at her nipple through the silky material and she thrust her crotch against my knee, hands twitching as she grabbed for the sheet that covered the mattress.

I could take her right then, jerk the leggings off and drive in. Bury my cock inside her. It ached and throbbed to do that very thing.

And yet I rolled half away, hooked my thumbs in the waist of her leggings and pulled them over her hips, then lower, as the material rolled across the narrow line of hair that disappeared between her legs.

I gave her a cheeky look and lifted my left eyebrow.

She couldn't meet my eyes.

"Every inch of you is a new surprise."

"Shut up," she mumbled on a gasp as I ran the tip of one finger down that line, stopping just before she parted for me.

I laughed and watched her writhe against me in the semi-dark. Still mostly dressed, hair a mess over the pillows, chest rising up and down as fast as my heartbeat, she was the sexiest thing I'd ever seen. No, the way her wet lips parted with excitement was the sexiest.

"I'm going to make you come, darlin. When you do, I want you to say my name."

"Cam." She gasped half breathless.

"Cameron," I corrected her. Nobody ever called me that and I couldn't figure out why I wanted her to so damn bad.

"Cameron." Her gaze caught mine, held it in the semidarkness.

"Yeah, baby, just like that."

Fifteen

Riley

My senses were heightened to a painful level. Even the throb of my pulse in my ears was borderline offensive. I wanted to scream, push his hand lower, beg him to undress me. I wanted things I'd never let myself think about.

Because I'd never met Cam.

And when he told me what he wanted to do to me, it was like having hot whiskey poured all over me. Sticky, warm, and intoxicating.

"Please."

With that wicked, provocative grin, he propped up on one elbow and pressed against my side. He pulled his hand from where it left heat at my cleft and licked his finger.

The lingering guilt vanished when he pressed that digit against my clit. I wanted this, didn't care what happened after. My journey didn't end here, but there wasn't any reason not to enjoy myself. I deserved that.

Besides, Cam brought me to life.

I closed my eyes against the sensation of the slow, gentle circles he made. I thrust my hips against his touch and gripped the sheets. Each time I moved, his erection rubbed against my thigh. Proof his desire matched mine.

"Cam." The word broke off as my body heaved, pleasure filled pressure building inside me.

Faster and faster his finger moved, then he stopped, slid one digit inside me and massaged the core of my pleasure with his palm. He stroked me inside with his finger, before turning his mouth to mine, sucking my bottom lip between his when I moaned. The combination of his sexy kiss and intimate touch was delicious torture.

It was too much. Sensations warred with each other. The taste of him was potent, consuming. And then he shifted his hand again, so that his finger made rapid, feather light movements on my clit.

My body pulled tight and I jerked from his kiss, gasping. "Oh. Oh. *Cameron.*"

Everything inside me exploded, warmth flooded from the core of me and toward his hand, my entire body wracked with the shocks of my first orgasm.

Nothing had ever felt so good.

He chuckled against my ear, the sound vibrating through me while I trembled with the aftermath.

"Told you so," he whispered as he rolled away to sit on the edge of the bed.

I had come saying his name, and everything had felt so completely right I couldn't help but want more.

"You say the word and this is as far as this goes." His voice was sleepy, his tongue thick with arousal. The sort of sound that forced me to roll toward him, run my fingers between his shoulder blades and down his back.

He'd touched me, but I'd not yet really touched him. The idea was more thrilling than anything ever had been.

He turned on the bedside lamp. "When I take you, I want to see you."

Sitting up, I tugged off my shirt. I could be shy, but not now, not with him. Whatever he wanted, I'd give him. Anything. My bra came next and there was a crinkle of plastic.

Cam stood long enough to slide off his boxer briefs. This time I didn't look away.

"Nice ass."

He snorted a laugh and turned to me. Then everything stopped. I held my breath as his blue eyes went dark, his mouth parted softly, and he bent to grip the edge of the bed. It was like he was drinking me in, memorizing every part of me.

My hands itched to pull the blanket up, cover myself. Instead, I laid back and pulled my knees up, parting my legs for him.

"Fucking hell," he growled and climbed on the bed with me. "Do you have any idea what you're doing to me?"

I glanced down at his arousal, straining against the condom, and my heart raced. Desire swallowed whatever fear I had.

As Cam crawled between my legs, he kissed me. There was nothing soft, nothing gentle. This kiss was fierce and scalded all the way through me. He broke the kiss as he slipped two fingers inside me, then back up to the source of pleasure that still hummed from his touch.

I gasped as he pulled one nipple between his lips, sucking it until it swelled taut and ached, and then moved to the other. I moved beneath him, grabbed his sides, and clung to him.

"I want..." I gasped as the tip of him pressed into me, opening me. "More."

Cam groaned and shifted, releasing my nipple and raising over me. He gripped beneath my knees, pushed them back against my chest, then slipped inside me.

I cried out, not from pain, that was momentary, but from the overwhelming clash of sensations. The muscles in my thighs pulled taut, tightening me around the width of him.

"Riley," he murmured and moved inside me.

The sound of skin on skin, the feel of him inside and the friction that built, consumed everything. Nothing else mattered but Cam and the way he made me feel. Every inch of my body was on fire, each thrust pushing me further into oblivion.

I don't know how long it lasted, but wave after wave came, pleasure and sensation continued to build as my body grew damp and I couldn't do much more than moan.

I came again, gripping the sheets as he thrust faster, until he released my legs and collapsed with a moan on top of me, his face buried in my neck.

It was several long minutes before I could form a coherent sentence. "Does it always feel that good?"

"Darlin." He half choked on a laugh, rolled his weight off me, and curled at my side. "If it doesn't, I'm doing something wrong."

"What about me?" I traced a finger down his chest.

"Fucking perfect."

Sixteen

RILEY

Riley

The loud, resonating rumble of a Harley throttling up the driveway broke through the fog of sleep. It was dark now. We'd slept most of the day, wrapped up in each other. Cam kissed the back of my neck before sliding from the bed and padding naked to the window.

I openly watched, enjoying the view of lean muscle as he peeked out the blinds before coming back.

"It's Merc." He flipped up his phone and checked. "Fuck. I slept through his calls."

"I didn't even hear the others leave." I stretched beneath the sheet, enjoying the slight soreness between my thighs. I wasn't a virgin anymore. One glance at Cam and I knew I could have picked a worse first time.

Cam grinned, flicked on the light, and leaned over the bed enough to kiss me. Gentle and chaste turned quickly into something else as I tugged him closer. "You're going to get me in trouble." He pulled away and yanked on a pair of jeans.

"How's that?"

Something in my question stopped him. He stood there and tilted his head, studying me as if he didn't quite know how much to say. He chose to let the silence linger and turned back to his dresser. I didn't like the way he didn't answer, the way some dark cloud hovered over him all of the sudden.

We'd been intimate, slept together. How was I going to get him in trouble? "What's going on? What are you not telling me?" I scrambled from the bed and got dressed. It felt like I needed armor to have this conversation.

He was pulling a white t-shirt over his head by the time I'd rounded the foot of the bed. "Wait in here. I'll be right back."

"No." I was trembling, but not from fear. "If this..." I gestured between him and the bed. "...is a problem, I need to know so I can make sure it doesn't happen again." Hot, mad tears threatened.

He sucked his bottom lip into his teeth and narrowed his eyes, his jaw tight. "I'm not asking you to hide from Merc."

"Aren't you?"

He stalked across the room so fast I didn't have time to brace myself when he pulled me against his chest.

"No. But whatever he's coming here to say to me, he ain't going to say in front of you." He looked down at me, lips tight. "Just give me ten goddamn minutes, okay?"

The strength of him pressed against me, shoved away all the other emotions. His body was warm, mine responded, and I held myself perfectly still to keep from rubbing against him like some sex starved groupie.

"I deserve to know what I'm getting into."

He released me with a sigh and two loud, firm knocks sounded on the door.

"We can talk about it later." And he walked out, in bare feet, pausing long enough to grab his smokes before shutting the front door behind him.

I wasn't hiding because he was ashamed of me, I told myself as I padded quietly into the living room. I was hiding because I was nosy. The past week had moved fast, different from the steady trod of screwed up news my life had been before.

It was messed up that a man had to die for my life to get better. The guilt churned away in my stomach. I shouldn't be enjoying any of this and yet...

Screwing up my nose, I knelt on the arm of the gray couch and leaned toward the window. I could make out their lower halves through the blinds, but just barely. Merc had walked to the railing and they both stood there, talking.

Club business wasn't any of mine, and I knew I shouldn't be skulking about trying to listen in. Halfway to standing, convinced to go back to the bedroom and mind my own 'business, I heard my name.

But if it's about you...

"She should be asleep." Cam said. "She seems to be doing alright."

"I bet." I couldn't see him, but the sarcasm in Merc's voice was clear.

"Is it a problem?" Something cold and hard snaked into Cam's voice, making my skin heat.

Would I always have that sort of reaction to him, or was it just because we'd had sex?

"Nah, man." Merc's ambivalent tone said, *I don't care.* The railing creaked, like he'd leaned against it. "I like her."

Good, because I liked him too.

Cam mumbled something I couldn't make out. I pressed my body against the door now, listening hard.

"You trust her?"

"Enough." Cam's answer was quick and noncommittal.

That stung. He trusted me enough to have sex with me, to sleep in the bed with me.

"Preach is real interested." Merc's words were so quiet I almost couldn't make them out.

But Cam's laugh rang loud and clear. "What the fuck about? Everything I've done since I was a teenager has been for the fucking club. That shit ain't changed. He's paranoid."

"Any reason to be?"

"Maybe."

More mumbles I couldn't make out, which left me time to question what Preacher would be after Cam about. Could Cam have something on him? Should I be concerned about Cam?

"Talked to Ky tonight." Merc's voice was hushed, but I could make it out. "He's got girls that work that motel we found Archer at, wants to know if he needs to be concerned."

"He doesn't."

Dylan had told me Archer's death was an apparent suicide. This motel stuff would probably be something else Cam was keeping from me. Maybe I should put it on the list to ask the lawyer about.

Who was Ky? As much as I wanted to listen, to find out more about how Archer died, I went back to the bedroom then. There was a cold, haunting tone in Cam's voice that I wanted nothing to do with. A reminder that here, with these people, I was out of my league.

When Cam came back in, I was flipping through social media photos of high school acquaintances. I hadn't posted anything since Mom's funeral announcement. There hadn't been anything to say. And now?

There's too much.

I ignored all the questions that burned my tongue more than I ignored him, waiting until I could no longer hear Merc's bike before saying anything. "There are a few things I really need to know." I stood, feeling like doing so made me seem more assertive.

"Alright." He leaned against the dresser. I tried not to notice the way the thin material of the t-shirt pulled tight around his biceps as he crossed his arms over his chest.

"How am I going to get you in trouble?" That was the easy one. Or should be.

He grinned, unfolding his arms and shoving his hands into his pockets. "Darlin, even now I want to throw you back on that bed for the rest of the night, bury my face between your thighs, and stay there until neither of us can say a fucking word."

As he advanced, I scurried backwards until the mattress hit the back of my knees and I sat on reflex. When he said it like that, the mental image made my mouth, and other things, water. I couldn't even remember my question.

He was going to do things to me that I never imagined.

Cam kissed me, his lips hot and urgent, tasting faintly of the menthol cigarette he'd smoked. Jesus, how was that even hot? Losing myself in his kiss made
it easy to forget everything except where I was and who I was with. It was as if my
very being was consumed by Cam the second his tongue brushed against mine.

But he'd said we'd talk and we weren't talking.

Nothing pissed me off more than being placated. Dylan's words about how
we weren't allowed to know things, still played in my head.

Cam was an expert at distraction. Making out with me, hovering over me,
and leaning me back on the bed. All of this was his version of a magician's trick,
outlaw biker sleight of hand. I wasn't about to fall for it again, no matter how
good he tasted.

I pressed my hand to his chest and pushed. Cam moved, pulling away and
straightening, closing his fingers around my wrist. His thumb stroked an absent
rhythm over the top of my hand.

"Did Archer really kill himself?"

There was a flash of acknowledgment, a brief lightening of his blue eyes
that told me he didn't think so. Not that he thought Archer wasn't capable of
suicide, but that something bigger was going on here.

I grew cold, my desire rapidly abating. Pushing past him, I collected my bag.
"I'm going to go back to the house."

"Why's that?" The annoyance on his face creased his brow but did little to
dampen his appeal.

I shrugged, shouldering the bag. "Because this was a bad idea."

"Darlin, everything about me is." His voice was tired, resigned, and stopped
me before I could walk out of the room.

"My mistake."

"Was it?"

No.

"I don't know. I can't figure out what you want from me. You won't tell me
anything, but you take me to meet a woman Archer was close with, someone
important. You boss me around and then make love to me." I turned to him,

frustrated and fed up. "Having sex with you wasn't the mistake, thinking you thought more of me than Krystal or one of the other groupies was."

"I do." He pushed his hand through his hair and shifted around the dresser. If I'd given him room to pace, he probably would have, but I blocked the door. "There are parts of my life I can never tell you—that I won't bring you into. Hell, you barely know me, much less *this life*."

"But some of it is about me, directly affects *me*."

"Like what?" There was a flash of vulnerability on his face when I took another step back, almost fully in the other room now.

He followed me, filling the doorway until I backed into the room. It was like an oddly sexy game of cat and mouse. If I ran for the door, would he run after me, grab me, jerk me against his chest again? Or would he stand there and watch me go?

I hated myself because I hoped he'd chase me and was tempted to find out.

"Are you serious? Someone broke into the house I'm staying in. I could have been there, alone. If you think someone murdered Archer, I deserve to know. It means something could happen to me too now."

His entire body turned to steel. "I'd never let anything happen to you."

"You're not invincible, Cam."

"You think I can't protect you?" He pushed his hand through his hair again and cussed under his breath. "Shit is sideways right now, both inside the club and out. But the one thing I know—I'd kill someone before they got close to you."

I balked at the passion in his voice.

"Trust me, darlin, you ain't been alone yet. You wouldn't have been."

"Even with your two...friends here?"

His face darkened. "Even then."

He was in front of me, long fingers tilting my chin up before I could prepare myself for his touch. "You feel it, too, don't you? You know damn well I was thinking about you the entire time. That's the problem, sweetheart. I need to think, to figure it all out. I can't when I'm with you, inside you. Everything goes away but you."

Whatever argument I'd had, whatever I'd been upset about, vanished. I trembled, standing there.

"I promise you. There's never been another woman that got inside my head like you. It's dangerous. I'll do whatever it takes to keep you safe. Hear me?"

Every word.

He kissed me, softly sucking my bottom lip in between his before snaking his tongue into my mouth. He plundered, taking with his tongue dancing around mine. I dropped the bag and clung to his hips. The kiss making it so easy to forget the things Merc had said on the porch.

I wanted to know more about how Archer died, but this wasn't the way to find out.

He pulled away, breathing heavy. "*We* can go back to the house. Until I find out who broke in, figure this all out, I'm keeping you close."

I nodded. He'd get no argument from me. I was relieved that he wouldn't let me go back alone. No matter how weak that made me feel.

I steadied myself as he collected his stuff and shrugged into his cut.

"What happens if your club finds out we slept together?"

He grinned. "Nothing. Except Jester can't flirt with you anymore."

At the door, he dropped a soft kiss to my lips. "Tomorrow night AP's cooking lasagna at his place. Wanna go?"

"Like a family dinner?" Those words put me in the mind of thirty-minute sitcoms, where families gathered around a kitchen table in some off-color kitchen to complain about the day. Cam didn't fit into that mold; none of them did. I lifted my brow as he opened the door and held it for me.

"Fewer people than at the clubhouse. We eat, have a few beers. No groupies." He pulled the door shut behind me. "I can't tell you everything, not now. But..."

He could give me this part of himself. I was good enough for family dinner. "You mean I can come out of hiding now?" It was a low blow, but no matter what he said, I was still running on high emotions. No one told me confusion and anger could be byproducts of my first orgasms.

"Ain't my place to tell anyone shit about you." He stopped at the bottom of the steps and shoved his belt through the loops of his loose fitting, dark wash jeans. "You want everyone in town to think we're fucking—I'm all for it. But I don't kiss and tell."

His smirk was as hot as it was annoying.

"I never know if I want to hit you or kiss you." The railing creaked when I leaned against it, stopping short of groaning or hitting him.

"Yeah, I have that effect." He eyed me up and down. "But if you want to skip dinner and spend the next few days alone with me, I'm all for that, too."

I couldn't help but laugh and blush a little. "To be honest, AP's lasagna sounds great."

Anything to put distance between what he'd just done to me, what I wanted him to do, and the secrets that were piling up.

***

Full access to a private bathroom was one of those weird things people take for granted. I did, for sure. Until I'd spent time living out of my car and only showering at the gym.

My makeup was spread out across the counter. I'd used my hair straightener, and it was put up on a shelf with my styling products. Maybe not mine, but Archer's house was starting to feel like somebody's home. Or at least a place where I could pretend—if only for a little while.

Cam and I had spent almost twenty-four hours pretending. Not much of that time talking. And I was okay with that. Making love to him, again and again, was as thrilling as the first time. Then we'd slept late, and he'd made me breakfast.

If I stopped to think about it, then deep down, it all felt wrong. Because I wasn't supposed to be here, wouldn't be here long.

Our lives were very different.

I was faking a lot of things. Well, not *one* thing. I still didn't know what to do with it. Cam Savage wasn't anyone's boyfriend, but I'd never considered myself the type of girl who just...did things like that.

I wasn't exactly a girl anymore, either. I was a grown woman. And as such, could do whatever the hell I liked with my body. And I'd liked that a lot. Too much, probably. And intended to keep doing it so long as I was here.

That thought was thrilling in a way I hadn't expected, making me warm and tingly all the way down to my toes.

Evenings cooled off quickly, so I wore a short, cropped short sleeved shirt that showed off about an inch of bare stomach before the hem of my high waisted jeans.

Cam waited for me on the carport, leaned against the seat of his bike, legs stretched out and crossed at the ankles, smoking a cigarette and scrolling through something on his phone.

Cam's slow look started at my feet and traveled all the way to meet my gaze. The warm, sexy flicker in his eyes was both a reminder and a promise. I shivered with anticipation about six seconds before silent awkwardness settled over me. Unsure what to do with my hands, I shoved them in my pockets.

He hadn't said specifically that I was riding with him. I'd assumed, because I wanted to. And now he was looking at me expectantly.

"Am I following you? I wasn't sure, since I've never been to APs, I didn't know if we were going together—"

"We'll ride." He rubbed his lips together, half distracted, and stood. "Wait here."

He made quick work of the steps up to his apartment and came jogging back down them quickly, something black and leather in his hand.

"Let's try this." He held out a worn, short jacket. There'd been patches on it at one time. You could see the small indentions where they'd been sewn on.

I moved, allowing Cam to slip it over my shoulders, and then spin me around to zip it. The weight of the leather was heavy, and it smelled cool and woodsy. It was a little long, hanging to my pockets and just over my thumbs, but it fit.

"Whose is it?"

He ran his knuckles down the front of it, his face quiet. Almost like he wasn't sure what was happening. "Mine. Yours now, darlin." He stepped back to examine his handy work and this time, whatever had bewildered him was gone.

"Thanks." I didn't tell him about the tingling sensation in my chest. Neither of the two women he'd booted from his apartment last night were wearing anything of his. But I was.

With a tie I pulled from my pocket, I twisted my hair at the nape of my neck as he put the helmet on me. The swing of his denim clad leg over the bike was sexy. Pretty much everything he did was. I climbed on behind him and settled onto the seat.

Seventeen

Riley

Each ride was different, but the tingling sensation when I pressed against him was constant. This time was slower, cruising through Dry Valley, not blazing down the highway, the rush of exhilaration ripping the breath from my lungs.

I relaxed behind him, hands on my knees, and took the time to check out the revitalized downtown district. The evening was late enough that most storefronts were dark. But there were enough bars and restaurants that steady foot traffic filled the sidewalks.

The roar of Cam's bike echoed off the brick buildings that butted up against mountains on one side. The reverberation drew attention. Awe from the teenagers, envy from the men, and something else entirely from the women.

I understood. Cam Savage had that effect, with his slicked back blond hair, short on the sides, lanky denim-clad legs, and dark blue plaid flannel shirt. But it wasn't the handsome face that got the attention. No, it was the smug arrogance. He knew people watched, and he didn't give a shit.

And this was the biggest turn on of all. When he caught me watching him through the mirror, he winked.

As we continued on, I noticed other things. The cop that didn't even look up when we passed, and the gold and black stickers on some of the storefronts...Desert Kings logo and all.

AP's house wasn't out in the desert like the clubhouse, or in one of the tidy neighborhoods like Archer's, but right on the edge of downtown. There were trees here, and grass in places. The neighborhood was older and with a good deal more character than Archer's. This was the sort of place where the homes spanned generations.

A few kids played out in a yard. All of them glanced up as Cam rolled down the street and pulled into a long, large driveway.

Several vehicles were already there. I recognized Dylan's Jeep and relaxed. I didn't feel so out of place when she was around. The feminine energy was appreciated. Cam rode past the cars and turned around in a wide area at the top, leaving his bike beside several others facing outward.

He backed the bike in a lot, as if he was always ready to make a quick getaway. Maybe he was.

That thought left a prickle up the back of my neck. Each time I started to feel a sense of normalcy in Cam's world, something popped up to remind me of all the frightening tales Mom had told me. Each time made it harder to convince myself she was just trying to spook me.

I followed Cam through the tidy backyard and up the back steps, through a laundry room, and into the kitchen. Instantly, the scent of garlic and pasta sauce wrapped me in a fond memory. I'd went to an Italian restaurant in the city with Mom a few times, but those aromas didn't even come close to this.

My mouth watered and my stomach growled.

"Dad made lasagna," Dylan called from the stove, over the bluesy music and laughter that trickled in from the other room. "He put tables out in the living room, too."

I was about to ask if she needed help, and then AP stepped into the room, oven mitts on his hands. The fluffy green gloves looked out of place on the denim-clad, scruffy man.

"What's happening, kids?" He grinned, but then looked from me to Dylan. In that one look, a thousand different questions passed.

I was eager to know what they were. Cam didn't seem to care at all. "Not a damn thing. But I'm about to rip into that lasagna, old man."

Merc slipped in behind his dad, a beer in his hand, and the corner of his mouth twisted up beneath the facial hair in an uncharacteristic grin.

Cam narrowed his eyes. "What?"

Merc's face exploded with a smile that could light up the entire desert on a moonless night. He should really do that more. "Deke's out."

Cam whooped, stopping just shy of jumping into the air before he stormed past Merc. I followed so far as the doorway, to see Cam wrapped in a back slapping bear hug with a guy that looked like he'd been a biker for longer than I'd been alive.

Dishwater brown hair, threaded with gray, pulled back in a ponytail. Tall and slender, with faded jeans that were almost too big. Beside him stood a mousy woman with a smile that hinted at her former beauty. Now, she just looked tired and relieved.

"I'm sorry I wasn't here." Dekes, I assumed, murmured into Cam's neck.

"Don't be. You're here now, brother."

"Who's this?" The man settled his kind brown eyes on me, over Cam's shoulder.

"Riley." Cam turned to me, grinning and waving me to him. "Come meet Dirty Dekes."

"Call me Dekes, or Frank if you want. This is my old lady, Shannon." I shook her small, but warm hand before he tilted his head sideways. "Do I know you?"

His wife jabbed a bony elbow into his side and raised both her eyebrows in that *I already told you this* way of wives and girlfriends.

"Archer's girl?"

"Seems so."

"Well then!" He scooped me up in a big hug. "Sorry for your loss, kid...but good to have you here."

And unlike with Preacher, Dekes seemed genuine and, in truth, it felt like he might be family.

***

The lasagna was delicious. Savory sauce covered pasta that practically melted with each bite, all wrapped up in gooey cheese. I ate until my stomach hurt. Considering how few hot meals I'd had the past few months, that didn't take long.

But I had a chance to study Cam in his element. Guard down, belly laughs, two plates of food. Dekes, apparently, had been a big influence on his life in the club.

Others had joined AP's family seated around folding tables in the great room. Puck and Jester were here. Puck's son, barely more than a toddler, rolled trains around beneath his table. Every so often he'd sneak grins highlighted in red sauce in my direction.

There was a family feel, an easiness that was missing at the clubhouse. Even I relaxed, enjoying a glass of wine as Cam's face lit in a big smile to some jail story Dekes regaled us with.

"I tell you, kid, you damn sure don't want to go back. They ain't washed none of the pods since you were there."

"You went to jail?" I wasn't surprised, but the way Dekes watched me, he was itching to talk about it.

There was something cute and innocent in the way Cam's cheeks reddened when put on the spot. "Yeah, juvie here and then in Clark County a few years ago."

He pushed his hand through his hair and Dekes chuckled. "Don't be shy now, Savage. If you ain't going to tell your little girlfriend about it, I will."

"I'm not—"

He waved off my protest.

Cam, for what it was worth, reacted like a shy little kid, shaking his head and rubbing his hand over his face. Could he be any cuter?

"We were all in Vegas, doing the Casino shit during a bike week event. Cam got a little too hot handed, security got involved—"

"What's that mean?" I interrupted him, leaning forward with genuine interest.

"I was winning too much." The cockiness seeped back in and Cam straightened. "They thought I was cheating but couldn't prove shit."

"They saw you leaving that blond dealer's apartment the night before." Merc tossed a wadded-up napkin at him.

Cam swatted it out of the way. "You can't prove that either, brother."

"Don't need to." Merc leaned back with a snort.

"Can a man tell a story?" Dekes barked with playful exasperation.

"Please, I'm riveted." I didn't bother looking at Cam. I could feel his smile. Like something warm, it tingled across my skin and left me far too comfortable at his side.

There was a rush of pleasure when he draped his arm over the back of my chair and twisted a lock of my hair around his fingers. His touch, however innocent, made me hyper aware, and I almost squirmed.

"He mucks it up with security, breaks one guy's nose, knocks a table over, and hauls ass out of there. Jumping over shit, going full on parkour with stacks of chips in his hands."

Dekes paused long enough to kiss his wife as she left the table, bored with a story she'd probably heard dozens of times.

I cast a quick glance at Cam as Dekes continued. He was happy here, letting this man tell his story.

"Jumps on his hog, shoving chips in his pockets, those mother fuckers falling everywhere, some homeless guy scrambling around scooping them up—"

"I'm standing there, taking a smoke break, and trying to figure out why the hell the kid is tearing ass out of the parking garage, and then I hear the sirens."

"I almost made it." Cam chuckled.

"Almost only counts in horseshoes and hand grenades." Dekes flipped a toothpick into his mouth. "We follow behind the cops, breaking a hundred miles an hour outside of the city, just seeing if the kid could make it to the county line."

He leaned forward and shook his head. "He didn't."

When I glanced at Cam, he lifted his shoulders like, *what can I say?*

"Why not?"

Merc actually laughed, and Dekes' grin shone all the way to his eyes. "This idiot ran out of gas."

The entire room erupted into laughter, Dylan standing to clear plates even as she chuckled. Shooting Cam an amused grin I followed her with more dishes.

"Thanks, I'm glad you came," she said once we were in the kitchen.

I rinsed utensils and plates, passing them to her as she loaded the dishwasher. The aroma of garlic and marinara was slowly swallowed by the crisp, fresh scent of the dish soap she was soaking pots in.

"Me too." I glanced out through the door, Merc and Cam with their heads together whispering, AP at the end of a table, watching them all with a happy smile on his face. "This feels more like a home than anywhere I've ever been."

The corners of her mouth curled. "Yeah. Where'd you get the jacket?"

Her question caught me off guard, jerking me from the buzz of happiness I found myself caught in, and my guard slid back in place. It wasn't the question, so much as the almost robotic way she asked it.

"Cam gave it to me."

She turned to me, not smiling, but with a soft look on her face. "Be careful, Riley." She took a deep breath. "I really like you. And I love Cam. If he's happy, I'm always going to be happy. But riding on his bike, wearing his first cut...that's making statements with weight."

The earnestness in her gaze worried me.

Had I done something wrong? He'd said I wouldn't be trouble for him, but I couldn't help but feel like I'd stepped over some imaginary line. "I didn't mean to—"

She grabbed my hand. "You haven't done anything. But this life—there are rules, and I don't think he's telling you everything."

"All right, ladies. My turn!" A jovial voice bounded into the kitchen, interrupting us and leaving me tangled in so many questions I felt like a moth stuck in a web, flailing to be free—the vibrations calling the spider right to me.

Jester was carrying more plates. I stepped out of his way as he deposited them in the sink. Dylan busied herself with turning the dishwasher on.

"A real man washes his own shit," he told me, before carrying on solemnly. "Except his bike. He leaves that to babes in bikinis."

His salacious wink was so over the top, I laughed.

"She's looking a little dirty. You should help me out, Dylan." He twisted a towel and popped her on the ass as she turned away.

She snatched the towel before he could get her a second time and was practically growling when he jerked her close. "Not for a million bucks, asshole."

"Yo, get a room!" Someone tossed from the doorway.

But Jester's eyes had darkened, something changing in his facial features. Dangerous, sexy, and sucking out all the air in the room.

Dylan dropped the towel and stepped back. "No thanks." Then after a long pause, a challenge passed in the slight curl of his upper lip. "I don't like being told what to do, and I don't listen for shit."

He laughed, leaning against the counter, and watching her as she walked away. "She's got me all wrong. I like 'em feisty first."

Eighteen

CAM

I got itchy if she stayed out of my sight for too long. Even here. Which was fucking ridiculous. I was obsessing, acting like an idiot over a girl. Not something I'd ever done, but Riley was different.

She's in danger.

And there was that. There were things I knew for certain: Archer hadn't killed himself. He and Preacher had been fighting for months, but about what I couldn't ever be sure. My money was on the deal Preacher wanted with the rednecks.

Riley came back to the living area just as we folded up the last table, Merc carting one out under each arm. I'd have taken one from him, but the scowl on her face stopped me. The urge to know what had happened, to stalk into the kitchen and put my fist through someone's face, was so strong I took a step back from her. Gesturing to the front porch, I followed Merc out and lit a cigarette.

"What's up?" I took a long drag, focused on the swirl of smoke on my tongue and the burn in my chest. Anything to keep from acting like some idiot with a hard on. I'd brought her here on the back of my bike, wearing my leather—I'd drawn enough attention to *us*.

Because I wanted them all—every last fucking man in this county—to know she was mine.

She blinked up at me with those hazel eyes with flecks of green and gold and then shook her head as if to clear it. "Nothing. Just thinking." She looked down and grinned, like we were sharing some sort of secret.

I could eat her alive.

If she'd come to me, wrapped her arms around my middle like I'd wanted her to, I would have held her right there.

I'd barely known her a week. *Jesus.*

"About what?" I flicked the ash, watched the little ember float away and disappear into the night.

"This is the closest thing to a real family I think I've ever seen."

My chest tightened, pride making me stand a little straighter. "A shit load better than what I was born with."

She leaned on the rail, looking out into the small rock and shrub garden I'd helped Dylan plant a few summers before. "I had Mom, always thought that was enough until..."

"You didn't have anyone else." I finished for her when she trailed off. It was a sentiment I understood and the reason I'd clung so tightly to the Kings.

"It's never been easy like this."

"All of us aren't like this."

She caught my gaze, wrapped her arms around herself, and nodded as if she understood. But how could I explain to her when—if I did, I'd be going against the vows that had saved me? Turning my back on the only real family I'd ever had.

"Well, thank you for showing the parts of you that are."

I put the cigarette out on the rail, dropped it into the little bucket set in the corner, and then rolled the fading tension from my shoulders about the time AP cracked open the door. "Yo Savage, I need you at the Black Cat by midnight."

Black Cat meant putting my game face on. After what Merc had said about Ky's girls, I wouldn't be surprised if I had to answer some questions when I got there. Sure, the club needed to handle business, but Archer was barely in the ground.

AP's expression was solemn. "It's the kid. You know he won't deal with Preacher. I need the two of you, punk." There was truth in what he said about Ky. The younger Ukrainian got sketchy when Preacher was around.

Hell, I couldn't blame him.

"The Black Cat?" Riley's sultry voice licked at my attention. When I glanced back at her, she was looking at me with that never ending curiosity.

"It's a titty bar!" Dekes drunk shout cracked out of the screen door.

I sighed. "It's business."

"Sure, it is." But she was grinning.

I expected her to be jealous, to act out. She surprised me again and didn't.

"I'll get Dylan to drive you home and have someone hang out there until I get back."

"Okay." The teasing tone left her voice. "I'll be fine."

She didn't know our world like I did. Dylan could stay at the house, Puck and a few other guys outside.

I leaned in, almost brushing my lips against hers. It felt natural to kiss her like that. But the closer I got, the more my body heated, and I wanted to do more than drop a quick kiss. I wanted to mold her body to mine, kiss her hard and remind her of all the dirty things I was going to do to her when I got back.

There was a flash of knowing across her face and her cheeks turned a vibrant shade of pink as she looked away.

"Be safe."

Those two words, spoken as she glanced away, were almost my undoing.

Nobody had ever cared if I was safe or not.

Then she laughed. "No running from the cops and doing crazy shit."

She really had no idea.

"And go easy on the lap dances. I haven't had a real shot yet."

Or maybe she did.

***

The final pop of my exhaust echoed across the valley as I cut the bike off. Ahead of me, Merc was already hopping off his and shrugging out of his cut. The clubhouse was empty. The only sound was the hum from the flickering neon signage that hung on the sun-faded brick.

I followed him, hanging my leather on the back of a chair as we worked in silence, changing into a Rocky's HVAC t-shirt.

"I'm driving." He snatched the keys off the table right as Preacher's text rolled through on my phone. I rubbed at the hairs that prickle up the back of my neck and made the place behind my ear itch.

Be there in half an hour.

"Preacher?" Merc asked, before locking the clubhouse door behind us.

When I cut him a sideways look, he chuckled and fired up the work van. "He's not about to let that shit go."

Preacher probably thought he could intimidate the youngest Ukrainian into selling weapons to the rednecks. "Or maybe he's going to make a play over his head?"

Merc's skeptic, sideways glance said everything. "That's not going to happen."

"Nope." Ky wasn't someone to fuck around with. Sure, he looked slick and clean—but I wouldn't turn my back on him.

The van rattled over a pothole. The entire cab smelled like old copper. But there was nothing in the back except a few empty freon jugs that would rattle in their rack at every pothole we hit. We'd made this trip so many times in the last eighteen months I could almost pretend I was working on air conditioners from nine to five for a crummy pension.

And going home to a woman like her...

Something like fear jerked me upright before I settled into the passenger seat. My hands were sweaty, my mouth dry, and even the cool air blasting from the vents was blistering against my skin. I'd never expected to see my thirtieth birthday. Now I imagined a normal life with a woman I had no right to.

"You thinking the Preacher shit is going to go sideways?"

It could, but that wasn't why I suddenly felt like I was going to hurl.

"Nah." I lit a cigarette and despised the trembling of my fingers.

"Archer?" There were very few people who knew what I'd done, that knew the dark shit that lived in my past. Not that Merc would call me on it. He had his own in spades, but he understood what losing Archer meant to me.

When I didn't answer, his tone changed, surprised. "Something with the girl?"

The smoke curled out of the window when I cracked it. I focused on those gray swirls, settling myself, much like tracing burns in the carpet, gave me something to focus on when Mom would shoot up. That memory was a reminder of all the reasons I could never have a normal life with anyone, much less Riley.

Because then I remembered the years that followed, the darkness that lingered there.

I'd seen too much shit. *Done too much shit.*

We turned off the highway well before the bright lights of the strip.

When I'd met Merc, he'd just been Jace. AP's kid, the only one around close to my age. We were friends from the jump. Ride or die before our sixteenth birthdays. Underneath the dark beard and shaggy hair was a loyal bastard who tolerated zero bullshit.

Jace Merrick knew me almost as good as I knew myself.

"Don't know." I took a drag and tapped the ashes over the edge of the glass. "I'm still working it out." Translation: I'd tell him when I had something to tell.

"Might want to let her know if you aren't playing for keeps."

When I snarled at him and ditched the cigarette, he rolled his eyes and snorted a laugh. "It's all connected. Archer's gone, you're marking territory everywhere she goes, and pissing Preacher off. Let me know if I need to hop off this Savage train of self-sabotage."

Never failed that when he really wanted to have an opinion on shit, it was something I didn't want to fucking hear. "It's not like that."

"Then what is it?"

I thought for a minute. "Fuck. I can't explain that shit either."

He didn't push and for a long time we rode in silence, just endless moonlit highway broken up here or there by passing headlights in the opposite lane.

"Be careful."

That was the second time someone had said that to me in the past few hours. My response was a half-annoyed grunt.

The flickering lights of The Black Cat Gentleman's Club lit his face as we pulled into the parking lot. Even the beard didn't hide the hard line of his mouth. I hadn't told her shit, hadn't explained the rules. But I'd done it to protect her. I couldn't explain that to Jace, not yet. I'd have to leave him with his opinions.

I climbed from the passenger seat. Preacher and Band Aid, a burly guy with a baby face, were already waiting outside with Kyrylo Soletsky. The heir to the Ukrainian mafia had a baby face that would fool just about anyone.

But I knew better. The cheap grin as Preacher talked was fake as fuck.

"About damn time." Ky's smile vanished from his face but twinkled, real, in his eyes.

I slapped my hand into his and let him pull me into a back smacking hug.

"Looks good on you." He tugged at the front of my t-shirt. "Maybe I won't lose any of my girls to the back of your bike tonight." There was no accent to his English. He'd grown up in Vegas. But he switched easily to Ukrainian to issue a few curt commands as we followed him into the club.

The lights and smells were all familiar. They used to leave me feeling at ease, maybe excited. The dancers here were as hot as any I'd seen in the city. And yet, I could only think about Riley.

I locked gazes with Preacher as we ducked off into Ky's office, and the spot behind my ear itched again. I let the older guy go in first, not trusting him not to knife me in the back. This was a brotherhood, with no place for that distrust and yet...

"The agreed-upon amount?" Preacher asked as soon as the door shut behind us. Asserting his dominance, an attempt to remind the younger men in the room he was in charge.

Ky nodded.

"Have you considered our offer?" Preacher barreled on, not giving him a chance to respond further.

Ky caught my gaze in the mirror across from his desk and made a face. Preacher was going over as well as a shovel to the skull. I'd not talked to Ky about this. Hell, I'd adamantly argued against Preacher's bullshit right alongside Archer.

"I have. My answer remains the same."

The tall Ukrainian looked at home in the dark wood and leather covered office. He wore all black, with the occasional flash of gold around his neck, in his ears, and on his fingers.

"Why not? White boy money spends as good as brown." The growl in Preacher's voice was meant to be threatening.

Ky considered a bottle of vodka, put it back, and poured shots of expensive tequila before turning and passing them out, purposely not answering. There would be no intimidating the guy who grew up with gangsters and war. He might live here, but he'd been home more than a few times.

Ky took his shot, swallowed, and smiled before hitching a hip on the corner of his large desk. "I don't shit where I eat. You shouldn't either."

I shot mine and dropped the glass on the sidebar. Preacher stopped short of scowling, but the man hated tequila—hell, his racist ass hated everything that came across the border. This was extra salt in the wound, not on the rim.

The grin I exchanged with Ky meant he knew it, too.

"Product is being loaded now." Then he looked directly at me, and any good humor egging on Preacher had brought to the room was sucked out. "For you, my friend, and in honor of Archer, my uncles have agreed on a good faith deal. Two days until we expect our payment—minus your cut, of course. The next run, we take half up front."

The ride I would make tomorrow.

Merc took a pointed interest in his shot glass. The vein in Preacher's neck throbbed visibly.

"Wait." Preacher folded his arms across his chest, his gut sticking out far enough he rested them on top of it. "I think I need to talk with Val."

"I'm curious why you think he'd entertain that conversation?" Ky's left brow raised.

Preacher's jaw clenched, forcing his handlebar mustache to raise like he'd just stepped in shit. I covered my chuckle with a cough and wiped a hand over my mouth. Our money stopped at Ky. The only one in the room who had ever spoken to any of his uncles about business was Merc.

"Because I think a renegotiation is in order."

Ky's shoulders went rigid like a fighter just before the bell. The four of us fanned out around him. But I wasn't fooled. We didn't have the high ground here. "None of my uncles will negotiate. Not for you, not for the goddamn president."

The door pushed open, a large body shouldered right behind Band Aid, then another, evening the odds.

"Let's chill," I interrupted, both hands up for peace. And then to Preacher. "This deal was already made in good faith, already set up with the buyers." *You don't want to piss them off.*

I wasn't about to get beat down by Ukrainian mobsters because Preacher wanted to measure his dick. Merc stood closer to me, out of the immediate line of fire.

When I offered my hand, Ky grabbed my forearm and pulled me to him again. The Ukrainians were touchier than the cartel, for damn sure.

Releasing me, he turned to Preacher. "Two days."

His face tight with barely contained rage, the older man nodded once, slammed the shot glass onto Ky's desk with too much force and stormed out.

"My uncles *do* want to speak to you," he said low to Merc.

My friend rapped his knuckles against Ky's. "I'll make it happen."

"And make him understand, I won't sell local. Not to those methed-up hicks, and if he keeps it up, not to the club either."

"I hear you, brother." I bumped his fist with mine and went out into the club.

Preacher's shit was going to boil over for Merc if I didn't put a stop to it. There were things Merc didn't like to think about—much less talk about. A part of his life that was darker than selling cluster bombs and other explosives to the cartel. Not to mention the cartel weren't the only ones who got weapons from the Soletskys.

It's how the Kings protected our part of the desert.

Fuck.

When he wasn't right behind me, I turned to see him watching a dancer on the main stage. She wore a blue wig and little else. I looked away before he did. Had I not had another woman on my mind, I might not have.

"Know her?"

Merc snapped his head up and out of whatever trance he'd been in. "Nah, but...she looks familiar."

"Don't they all, brother?" I smacked his shoulder with a laugh. And with that, we walked out.

Nineteen

Riley

Watching Cam and Merc ride away from the house left a tug of longing inside me. How could I miss a guy I hardly knew? If I thought about it, it was almost embarrassing how a few bouts of sex left me feeling like a clingy, hormonal teenager. I was a smart, independent woman. Wasn't I?

Of course you are.

This was crazy. Yet the pit in my stomach was only trumped by the excited ripples of anticipation that he'd come home. The promises of the dark, of Cam, were enough to force me to swallow hard while standing in AP's kitchen.

"You ready?" Dylan gave me an easy smile when she came back in, stopping to drop a kiss to her dad's cheek. "Puck and Drop Top are at the house already, playing cards on the back patio."

"Don't let them get too drunk."

She scrunched her nose. "Puck barely drinks."

"It's not him I'm worried about." He snorted.

"True. Love you."

"You too." Then to me. "Take care, Riley."

"I will. Thank you for inviting me."

There was a softness to AP in that moment. Beer left his eyes red rimmed and took the edge from the way his lips curved. Here was home. He was just a man watching his daughter and her friend get ready to leave after a happy night with his family. The gangster, wild ass biker, was gone, the family man in his place. I could see him bouncing grandchildren on his knee with candy in his pockets.

Had I been raised here, known my father, AP would be that protective uncle I'd never had. Something in my heart swelled, and I stopped to give him a quick hug.

"You're always welcome here, kiddo."

I choked back the tears as he hugged me back and hurried out of the house before I cried. Family, like this, was something I'd never experienced. All of it was new, fresh, and flying at me all at once.

"He likes you."

I glanced back at the house as Dylan directed me to a shiny, new, white Jeep with the doors and roof pulled off. "I like him. AP's nice and makes me feel like I could belong here."

She stopped with the hood of the white Jeep between us. "I wasn't talking about my dad."

***

The ride home, as that's what Archer's house was beginning to feel like, was a somber one. I felt like everything had been going well, and now Cam's words echoed back to me. *You're going to get me in trouble.* I couldn't shake the feeling that there were things they weren't telling me. Before we walked under the carport, I stopped. Puck and Drop Top played cards at the table near the back door, and the faint scent of weed wafted to the driveway.

"Is something bothering you?" Genuine concern made my chest a little tight. It had been years since I had a real girlfriend. I hadn't kept in touch with anyone from high school. By the time Mom got sick...there was just too much distance to conquer.

"Cam's being sketchy, has been since you got here. I thought at first it was grief, but now I'm not so sure." She took a deep breath, looking anywhere but at me.

"He's got you on the back of his bike during an MC thing, has you wearing his first leather to family dinner." She worried her bottom lip. "Cam's never made that sort of statement."

An unexpected pressure settled on me. I wasn't stupid. Other women around the club were more experienced, had more to offer him than I did. I wasn't a Krystal or any of her friends. But now I felt like maybe I needed to be.

I was stumbling through all of this the best I could.

"I told you, around here, things are different. You're wearing something of his, on his bike—you're his property. It makes you his old lady. It's just the way things work here. Guys pass the groupies around. But an old lady? You don't fuck with an old lady. No one does."

There wasn't anyone else I'd want to mess around with, not now.

But there was more here, a lot she wasn't saying.

The secondary set of rules and laws these people lived by made my brain hurt. But somewhere inside, the thought of that thrilled me. He'd chosen me.

"Do you have feelings for him?" The question was quiet.

I didn't immediately respond. The truth was, my answer was terrifying. Yes, I had feelings. I didn't understand them, not yet, but it wasn't Cam they were going to be a problem for.

"Cam puts on a good show, but he's not like some of the other guys. The life he lived before the Kings was...bad."

That she knew things I didn't, stung. They'd been friends for years; I'd only known him a few weeks. But I'd shared my trauma with Cam. I'd never seen past his patch, past the mask of indifference. Other than what little Ro had told me.

"And you're just going to leave." Dylan's tone was so stiff and angry I flinched against it.

"I haven't made a single promise to him." It was all I had to offer. Even if tonight had been the first time I'd felt connected to anywhere since Mom died, Dry Valley wasn't my home.

"Have you slept with him?" She pushed a little too far.

Pissed off now, my jaw tightened, and my nostrils flared. "That's none of your business. And even if it was, we're talking about a man that a few days ago was having a go at two random groupies in his apartment."

She recoiled like I threw something at her.

"For what its worth, I'm not some femme fatale sent to destroy his life and make a mockery of your world. Hell, until I came here, I was a virgin."

"I didn't mean..." She faltered and screwed up her brow.

"Then what, Dylan? All I've heard now is all the things I'm doing wrong with a guy I barely know from a woman who doesn't know me at all."

"He's got a lot to lose with all of this." No stuttering there, she said it with feeling.

"Until a few weeks ago, I was homeless. He's not the only one."

"All I know is I see someone I love gearing up to do something stupid." Defiance flared on her pretty face.

"He's a smart man. I'm sure he knows exactly what he's doing."

I stormed toward the door and turned to Puck, the large, muscled tattoo artist. "You can all get lost. I don't need babysitters."

He sighed, leaned back into his chair, and gave a solemn shake of his head. "Sorry, but you'll have to take that up with Savage."

I swallowed my scream of frustration and stormed inside. It was petty and childish, but I slammed the door before locking it.

***

I was lost in my own head. Right when I thought everything made sense...Cam happened. He was the storm that came through and blew apart all my carefully put together plans.

I wanted him to touch me again.

I wanted to strangle him.

Maybe both at the same time.

His presence was the sort of thing that could be felt before I heard him. Even now, though he was so quiet the floorboards didn't even creak, I knew he was in the doorway before I bothered to look up.

"Heard you gave my guys some shit." More tired irritation than accusation.

"I don't like being held captive."

"They gave you space."

"Yup." Pettiness meant I didn't look up, only stared at his worn dark boots and the faded jeans he wore. I stopped before I looked at the rest of him—didn't trust myself. He'd turned me into a puddle not long ago, and he could do it again. I wasn't that girl, even if I wanted to be.

"We going to talk about it?" He said it so low, I almost questioned if I heard right.

Cam was giving me an opening. I could shout and rave about how I felt. The problem was, I didn't know. Part of me was excited, part of me terrified, but really, but mostly focused on surviving the next few weeks with some sense of normalcy intact.

"I left your jacket in the kitchen." I had draped it across one of the kitchen chairs.

"It's yours. I gave it to you."

"Why?" This time I did look at him, caught his gaze and held it. Something sizzled between us as I sat on the bed and he leaned against the door jam.

He pushed his fingers through his hair and looked away, dropping his hand to massage the bend of his neck. He still wore the vest, the crisp Vice President patch standing out against the other faded ones. I focused on the bright white threads to keep from getting lost in the way his tongue ran across his bottom lip or how his chest heaved as he released a sigh.

It was like every little thing he did appealed to me.

"It's a jacket. You didn't have one." Clipped. Short. No nonsense. That was the end of that.

But I wasn't finished. I'd waited all night to clear all this up. "And bringing me to AP's on your bike?"

This time he caught my gaze. His eyes were icy, the cold running all the way through me. The sort of thing that would scare a normal person. Instead, I sat up on the bed, inching a little closer.

"Notice the way Preacher looks at you? How at the clubhouse, guys circle you like sharks?"

The old guy was a creeper for sure, some of the others too.

"Would you rather be a groupie? Be like Krystal, get passed around for a good time? Because if that's what you want, I'll take the jacket back."

"Oh." I had hoped...for something more after everything that happened between us. Which was naïve.

"If you'd rather ride with someone else..." He let that thought fall off with a lazy roll of his shoulder.

I narrowed my eyes. No, I didn't. But judging by the mischief that danced across his arrogant expression now, he knew it.

The insolent way he watched me as he lounged against the door frame was infuriating.

"This make me your old lady?"

"Is that what you want?"

I cocked my head to the side and pursed my lips, mocking him with my own bratty expression. I should be tired. The argument with Dylan had drained me. But the truth was, I wanted this. To be his old lady, at least while I was here.

Being with Cam was the most alive I'd ever felt. "If you're going to make me stand out, at least treat me like I earned it."

His red-rimmed eyes narrowed, and his upper lip curled just enough to flash his teeth. My heart sped up, tripping over itself so that I trembled. It didn't matter what label he gave me, the second he looked at me like I was good enough to eat...all bets were off.

Twenty

Riley

Anticipation squeezed all my muscles tight when Cam stood to his full height and crossed the room. He was going to kiss me. But more, he was going to touch me. I'd worn only a t-shirt and panties to bed. And instead of moving to cover myself when he got close, my knees opened, and I licked my lips.

It was as if my entire body had readied itself for him.

He smelled faintly of smoke and cologne, like he'd just come from a strip club. But he didn't smell like a woman.

His lips were demanding and he tasted of hints of vodka laced with something dark and sexy. I kissed him back, my tongue rolling against his as he used his body to push me back on the bed.

I shoved the cut off first, the thick leather hindering my ability to touch him. I wanted to *feel* his body, the muscles in his shoulders, down his back. And I did, raking my hands over them, then down his forearms, and beneath his shirt.

I'd never expected a man to feel so good, that I would be so aroused by tracing the muscles down his back.

Cam broke the kiss long enough to pull his shirt off and then mine, too. He stroked up my sides, cupped my breasts, and flicked his thumbs over the taut nipples.

The sensation was sensual torture, as was the way his blue eyes drank me in. I squirmed, gripping his hips and pulling him to me. He kissed me again, warm and wet and everything I could have ever wanted.

When I nudged him, Cam rolled to his back, allowing me to climb on top of him as he pushed his jeans and boxers down, and I wriggled from my panties. For the first time, I wrapped my hand around the width of his erection and stroked his cock.

The skin was silky soft, the muscle rock hard. The contrast so erotic that, for a brief moment, I considered wrapping my lips around him. Then he groaned, a low sultry sound that snapped my attention to the way pleasure twisted his face.

I shifted my grip, continued to fondle him just to watch him suck that plump bottom lip between his teeth.

His hands trembled ever so slightly as he leaned forward, nibbling at my neck and reaching behind me. When he fell back, he handed me a condom like a damn magician.

When I laughed, he grinned through rapid breaths. "What?"

"Where'd that come from? It's like sex magic."

He snorted and shook his head. "My pocket."

Maybe it was the delirium and lack of sleep, but he looked so damn cute, all baffled and confused. Still gripping his cock, I leaned forward and kissed him.

I'd watched him put a condom on before, so rolling that one on wasn't a problem. I didn't hesitate until I hovered over him, shivering but not from the cold, with the tip of his cock pressed against my entrance.

"I..." It was my turn to lose the ability to speak. Being naked, Cam's hands on my breasts, made me want nothing more than to slide down on him. But I froze, second guessing myself and what to do next.

Sex should be natural, should come easily, it had been when he'd been the one doing the work.

He knew, he always did, and his hands slipped to my hips. Cam moved beneath me, sliding his cock inside me fully, his hips shifting up and back down in a natural rhythm that arched my back.

My body reacted, instinctively knowing how to move. And I did, up and down until sweat formed down my back. Pressing my hands against Cam's chest as I rode him.

Pleasure built slowly now, my body tired, but it came. Ripples of friction that turned to waves until I was gasping in time with each thrust.

I whimpered his name and shut my eyes when he raised up to suck my nipples. First one, then the other, leaving me to move, to ride him.

I cried out when I came, no name, no words, just a guttural release after a thunderclap of pleasure. Cam's body tensed as he clamped down on his jaw, and his eyes rolled to the back of his head.

I'd never seen anything sexier.

"*Riley.*"

I'd never heard anything sexier, either.

***

I rolled onto my elbow as slowly as I could, gently sliding my legs from beneath the sheets. I'd waited to crawl from the bed until Cam had rolled away from me. I'd been awake close to half an hour. Not that I was trying to be sneaky, but I'd rather not wake him.

He'd spent the night curled around me, but now he slept hard flat on his back, one arm tucked behind his head and the other sprawled across the empty side of the bed. His face was completely relaxed, serene even. Our clothes lay sporadically on the floor between the door and the bed, his pistol on the night-stand.

Trust.

I could slap him, kick him, scream at him—even go for the gun, all before he woke. And he knew that, but he trusted me not to. Somehow, sleeping and completely vulnerable, he was even sexier.

There were so many questions. Did my father kill himself and if not, who had? And what did Cam really expect from me? What did I expect from him? I almost forgot them all when it was like this, as if I could easily spend every day waking up to Cam this way.

That left an ache in my chest I didn't want to think about, so I tucked it away in a neat little box in a tidy corner in the back of my mind.

I picked up his cut, hanging the heavy leather vest on the doorknob, before collecting my panties and shirt. To keep from waking him, I cleaned up in the hall bathroom and padded barefoot to the kitchen.

I was Cam Savage's ole lady. A far cry from going back to college, applying for law school.

I poured a cup of coffee and put it to my lips as I leaned against the kitchen sink. The hot, slightly bitter liquid scalded my tongue with the first sip. The brief flash of pain grounded me there in the kitchen when Cam sleepily trudged in, clad only in his form fitting boxer briefs.

"Morning," he said, groggily rubbing his face.

His heavy-lidded, sleepy eyes made me want to kiss him. So I did, cupping the side of his face and brushing my lips across his before glancing at the clock. "Afternoon."

"Yeah, we have to hit the road soon." There was something sneaky in his grin. He kissed me, this time deeper, his tongue tracing across my lips before diving in. And one hand slipping between my legs, stroking the tips of two fingers across the thin fabric covering my sex.

"We don't have time."

"We do," he insisted, placing my coffee on the counter and tugging my panties down.

And before I could say a word, he murmured, "Sex magic" and flipped a red wrapped condom between two fingers.

Turns out, we had plenty of time, on the counter by the window.

By the time Cam finished with me, I was breathless and my coffee cold.

"Do you not want me to go?" I could tell it bothered him that I was making this ride. He procrastinated as long as he could. Even trying to distract me in the shower.

His eyes narrowed, and he straightened, pulling a clean white t-shirt over his head. "If you don't, Preacher's going to insist you hang out at the clubhouse with him." He crossed the room to where I sat on the bed, pulling on my socks. "Unless that's what you want?"

There was a teasing to his tone, but I kept mine firm. "Absolutely not."

"Good." He kissed me, gently. "I've got to get some shit from my place. Meet me out back in ten minutes."

Twenty-One

RILEY

This go round, I was dressed the part. No more quiet, unassuming Riley. I wore a pair of high-waisted cutoffs, a red fitted tank, and shoved my feet into a pair of well-worn cowboy boots I'd had since high school. Hair braided in the back, I put on a pair of dark shades and shoved my phone into my pocket.

I drew a long, appreciative assessment from Cam when I stepped out the back door.

"You look good." That appreciation was thick on his tongue.

I fought not to respond. I wanted to lick my lips and crawl up his leg. I wanted him to make me feel the things only he could. It was like we didn't just have sex on the kitchen counter.

Damn.

He pushed the helmet on my head and gave it a gentle smack to make it fit snug. Then he tipped my chin as he tightened the strap. "If you'd rather not go, darlin, speak now or forever hold your peace."

Oh, I wanted to ride with him. There was nothing else in the world like it. The idea left my stomach tingling with excitement. But I was apprehensive. He didn't seem to want me to go, but why? Still too many secrets. When I didn't say anything, he leaned close enough the scruff around his lips tickled my cheek. "Have it your way," he whispered in my ear.

I clung to his sides as he throttled down the driveway and out of the neighborhood. He didn't drive like he was pissed, but there was force in each shift of the gears, and by the time we pulled into a rundown tire place, I could feel the tension radiating off of him.

There was an old gray van, with ladders and piping strapped to a rack on the roof. Rocky's HVAC emblazoned all over it. And Merc, dressed like he worked there on the regular, leaned against the side, dark hair pulled from his face in a half ponytail.

Cam lit a cigarette once he pulled in and killed the motor.

"Looking like you belong there." Merc grinned and jutted his chin toward me on the back of the bike.

I fought back the little thrill I got when he said it. like This feeling was new, and I battled that excitement each time someone looked at us as we rode through town. I drew attention. Not because I was pretty, or special, or worthy—but because I was on the back of Cam's bike.

"She does," he stated with a matter-of-fact lift of his left shoulder.

I shouldn't like that. I hated myself for it. Especially when I hadn't been given much of a choice.

Would it have mattered? Probably not.

"You go back to The Cat last night?" Cam asked, taking a drag of the cigarette he'd just lit.

I didn't know Merc well, but their relationship was definitely the tightest of them all. A lot was said in the silence before Merc spoke.

"Nah, I'll run out there in a few days, get all this shit out of the way, let the other blow over first." That hung heavier than Cam's question.

I was paying attention now. Whatever we were about to do held repercussions for both of them that had nothing to do with the act itself. Me riding with Cam was some sort of dog and pony show.

But for who?

I studied Merc. His dark wavy hair was too short for a full ponytail and would have hung shaggy around his bearded face. That same beard wasn't long, but full and dark, hiding a boyish grin. I'd seen pictures of him without it, almost too pretty, complete with dimple pale blue eyes.

Yeah, he knew he was good looking. But unlike Cam, he didn't like it—so he hid it. Or at least, that's what I told myself. There were tattoos on his arm, in Latin, with military insignia. This wasn't his first brotherhood, or maybe it was, and the other skirted the edges. Either way, I was pretty sure he earned his nickname.

There was a divide in the Desert Kings, the broken line of it hovered on the edges of my periphery. And whatever it was, had to do with my father.

Another bike roared in and slowed on the blistered and cracked parking lot pavement. Jester's hair pulled all the way back, leaving the tattoos up his neck and throat fully visible. "Party's here, let's roll boys. Deputy Dog Hayden gave the all clear."

I'd met a Hayden. I let the name roll across my tongue until I latched onto the memory. The local deputy who introduced himself at the funeral. Another cog in the Desert Kings machine

"Keep me out of handcuffs, brother." Merc rapped his knuckles against Jester's and crawled into the van. He stopped and peered at Cam, mirrored shades paused halfway to his face. "You stay out of them too."

Cam grinned, a beaming sarcastic show on his face. "She might like it."

I ducked my head and blushed when the other two guys laughed. I didn't look up until Jester fired up his bike and rolled out of the parking lot ahead of Merc in the van.

"He's not an air-conditioning guy, is he?"

Cam crushed out his cigarette and laughed. "As far as you know? He sure the fuck is."

When we didn't immediately follow, I caught Cam's gaze in the rearview mirror. "Are we going?"

"Nope." Cam checked his phone, before shoving it into his pocket. "I got something else to do."

I clung to his waist, more curious than I had been before, but no less excited about the ride.

***

Everything in my life needed a reason, a box to check, a slot to slide into. Everything except this. I leaned against the bar at the small of my back and turned by face to the sun, thankful for the dark shades that kept the wind from my eyes.

The sky was gorgeous, the mountains and rock formations were inviting, their reds and oranges splashed vivid color against the edges of the golden desert. Greenery periodically dotted the horizon, but we'd pass it so quickly I couldn't tell what dared grow here.

The roar of the Harley Davidson paired with the howl of the wind as we blew down the two-lane highway was freeing. Each time I rode like this with Cam, I lost something I didn't need and found another piece of myself I hadn't realized was missing.

Here, everything was thrust at me in full contrast. No questions. Right and wrong didn't matter. Life just *was.*

Cam squeezed my knee, running his palm up my outer thigh. His touch, a thread that seemed to wind through everything. A physical connection to the exhilaration that raced over me. When I left here, this is what I would miss the most.

Through the mirror, I glanced at Cam, the proud set of his jaw, the shape of his lips that made me want to lean around and kiss him. I'd never had those little urges, and I couldn't silence them, so I dropped my hands to my knees.

He stopped stroking me, reached behind him, took my right arm, and wrapped it around his middle. I couldn't see his eyes through the aviator shades, but I didn't need to. He wanted me to hold on. We were cruising now. I didn't need to—he wanted it.

I wrapped both arms around his waist, sliding my hands beneath the cut to brush against the cotton covering his stomach.

The half grin he shot me through the mirror excited me, aroused me even. I was wilder here, so was he.

I don't know how long we rode through the desert, but we were so far out that only the occasional gas station or dilapidated truck stop dotted the landscape. And then, after ten or so miles, those buildings came more frequently, followed by little neighborhoods with two of three streets of copy paste houses.

Cam decelerated as a shining silver bullet style diner appeared, swung into the parking lot, and pulled right up front.

"What are we doing?"

He grinned. "The pie here is amazing."

"That's a long way for pie." Dubious, I climbed from the bike, took off the helmet, and laid it on the seat. Thankful for the braid, it kept most of the tangles at bay.

"Best strawberry pie in Nevada."

Much like earlier, there was a big something I didn't know. Dylan's voice was in my head, reminding me that they didn't tell us anything, ever.

He held the door for me and a tired waitress waved for us to seat ourselves. Cam led me to a tight booth by the wall of windows. The seats were cracked and the tables were scratched and scuffed glass covering old Hayes County advertisements. The place was so packed, I didn't expect the server to make it to us anytime soon. But she surprised me, stopping by to take our order before I'd so much as settled onto the seat.

"Two coffees, two pieces of strawberry pie." Cam didn't even give her a chance to get menus.

When I gave him a look, he smiled in that cat like way he did to distract women. It still made me tingle, but I'd caught on to what he was doing. "We won't be here long, darlin, just a pit stop."

The coffee and pie came just as quickly. After my first bite, I realized Cam wasn't wrong. The crust was perfection, the chunks of strawberry fresh, and sweet filling not too sticky. I had to remind myself not to eat it all in two bites.

Cam, however, ate his slowly, more interested in the parking lot than the flaky crust. I watched too, as a steady stream of people filtered in and out.

"I'd hate to see this place during the dinner rush." I mused.

Distracted, Cam didn't hear me. Instead, he looked past me, toward the door, and gave a stiff smile before standing.

Two Hispanic men approached, both in khaki shorts and a light colored polo shirts like they'd just stepped off the golf course. The taller of the two's back was straight, his dark eyes flickered from one end of the diner to the other.

The other man moved like a cat, with the ease of concealed violence. His dark hair was cut short and glistened in the fluorescent light. He hung sunglasses through the buttonhole on his collar, and I was privy to sleepy eyes hooded with a thick curtain of dark lashes.

His toothy smile was almost predatory and he pulled Cam into a hug as I watched.

It was there, so smooth I'd have missed it had I not been watching so closely. There was no way anyone else would have seen it. But a thick envelope passed between them and disappeared inside Cam's cut. It made the hair prickle on the back of my neck.

"Savage, good to see you." He released him and turned to me.

All good humor vanished from Cam's face and stayed standing, proof there were at least two apex predators at the table.

"You must be Riley, Archer's daughter. I'm Santos Garza." He extended a hand, his expression warm despite Cam's warning glare. "My condolences on your loss. I was saddened to hear about Archer, I considered him a friend—and I don't have many of those."

I felt like I was tossed into The Godfather—Desert Redux and shivered despite the warmth of the crowded diner.

"Thank you, I appreciate that."

"And if you ever need *anything*, don't hesitate to give me a call. I owe Archer a few favors." When he released my hand he took a card from the other man and handed it to me. There was something in the way he emphasized the word *anything* that made me dizzy and panicked.

As if he sensed that, Cam tore some bills from the roll in his pocket and tossed them onto the table. "Good to see you, Garza, but we were heading out."

I hadn't even touched my coffee, but I didn't dare say that. Not when the tension around us was so thick.

Garza just smiled big like the Cheshire Cat as he backed from the table. "Tell your new president I need to speak with him on a personal matter."

"Will do." Cam pulled me from the booth and held my hand all the way to the bike. He handed me the helmet and leaned close, brushing his lips across mine before whispering in my ear. "When we get home, burn that fucking card."

Frazzled, annoyed, and more than a bit freaked out I climbed on the bike behind Cam. From inside, Garza looked out and saluted us with his coffee.

Cam turned to me a little bit. "He shouldn't have known who you were." Then he fired up the bike.

Judging from the tension in his body as I wrapped my arms around him, it was a miracle he didn't sling gravel all the way out of the parking lot.

Twenty-Two

CAM

We'd been on the road for fifteen minutes when I saw the rusted out, jacked up truck the first time. I couldn't get away from the prickling sensation on the back of my neck when I'd seen Santos had known Riley. That distraction meant I picked up the tail later than I should have.

Paranoia had me making several bullshit turns. I was thankful Riley wasn't familiar with the area. She already asked too many questions—I didn't want to scare her more.

Fuck me.

"What's wrong?" I could barely hear her shout over the roar of my bike.

We were being followed. The money in my vest throbbed hotly. I'd face ten different truckloads of rednecks trying to steal this shit before I'd show up empty-handed at The Black Cat.

And the cartel was worse. I should have never brought her, even if she had been a smoke screen. Nobody would notice a couple on a bike, eating pie in a diner. Hell, I hadn't expected Santos himself. That on its own was fucking bizarre.

My life wasn't made for someone like Riley. She could get hurt, or worse.

Guilt left me shaky, so I flexed the fingers of one hand and looked for a place to exit. Get her off the bike, back home safe, while I handled this.

The roar quieted to a throb as I let off the throttle and nodded toward a roadside bar with cars in the lot. I needed a public place to ditch Riley. "You hungry?"

Annoyance furrowed her brow as I deflected. It was better if she got a little pissed at me. I needed to get her out of here before she got attached—before I did. I was stupid to put a label on us. Santos had been a grim wake up to that fact.

But I wanted that one piece of peace, something untainted—and Riley was it.

Fucking stupid.

There were too many dangerous people sizing her up. Archer had been a fool bringing her here when he wasn't around to protect her. And me, an even bigger one. Sex had never done that to me before.

Two banged up pickups, with straight piped exhaust, sputtered past as I parked. The rednecks inside looking anywhere but at me. Yeah, right. I climbed from the bike and texted Merc while Riley took off her helmet and used the mirror to tame the auburn fly-aways.

"Let me guess, more *pie*?" The sarcasm that dripped from that last word made me want to simultaneously throttle her and kiss her.

"Nah, darlin, not here."

I held the door open for her and let it close behind us in the air-conditioned dark bar. As the heavy metal door closed, the junky truck pulled in, its exhaust coughing. She stole my focus, muddled shit up, and it had almost cost me.

The bartender was too preoccupied with his phone to notice us, so I chose a corner booth and sat facing the door.

I was on edge, thinking too much. I did that right before things went to shit, and I had a feeling they were about to.

I leaned back and threw an arm over the booth, made an executive decision. "I'm going to text and have somebody ride out and pick you up."

There was a subtle change in her expression. Her lips went tight for a breath. She straightened and then blinked. "Why? Because that guy gave me his number?"

With a nonchalant shrug, playing off my unease, I rubbed a hand over my mouth. "I've got some club shit to do."

"I can ride with you," she suggested, thumbing through the menu. "I thought that's what Ole Ladies did?"

"That's not the way it works, darlin. The MC takes precedence. Shit like this happens."

"I'll rip up the number, you don't have to be all jealous." She stiffened, crinkling the edge of the menu between her fingers.

Santos Garza and Riley made me feel a lot of things, but jealousy wasn't one of them. But right then I didn't have time for the petty girl drama.

I fired off a text to Merc.

Nonchalant again, keeping my voice from coming off too rigid, still trying not to spook her. "Darlin, I don't get jealous. Not when I could have my pick of any woman in the county. And some of them together, remember?"

The flash of outrage in her eyes told me to gear up for one hell of an argument. She'd never met Archer, but holy shit, the way her eyes widened was just like his. It reminded me of what we had to lose.

Riley was cut off by the waitress, whose ill-timed smile was as big as her fake tits. "What can I get y'all?"

My phone buzzed...Merc heading back to the clubhouse. Riley wasn't the only one gearing up for a fight. It'd be a while before Dylan or one of the other ladies made it out here.

To buy some time, I'd piss Riley off so she'd go no matter who showed up. I turned on every bit of my charm.

Women liked me, it was a fact I'd learned early on. If I gave them a half smile, leaned in like I did now, they'd all but hop in my lap. Desperate women, those who needed to feel like they still had it, made seduction even easier.

The over eager, forty-plus waitress was so close I nearly choked on her department store perfume.

"I can make some suggestions." They'd have nothing to do with the menu. She was the sort that thought she could show me a thing or two I'd never seen. She'd be wrong.

There'd been women just like her for more than a decade. I'd seen it all already.

I hazarded a sidelong glance at the ample cleavage she was trying to lure me with. Bitch had nothing on Riley, all the tits in the world didn't. I was more a quality rather than quantity man.

But Riley didn't know that. Her eyes had narrowed, her lips pursed. She may not admit it, but jealousy radiated off her in time with the music from the jukebox.

The waitress' caked-on makeup showed their twenty-year age gap. She bent further over the table, her tits almost falling all the way out. "I know what a man like you likes."

Not even close.

Riley glowered at her. We were in the middle of something bigger than greasy bar food and promiscuous waitresses, but she didn't seem to notice. For once her innocence frustrated me more than aroused me.

I shook a toothpick from the little container on the table and flicked it into my mouth. "What are you drinking?" she practically crooned as she hitched a hip on the table and kept her back completely toward Riley.

I spun the toothpick between my teeth, drawing her attention to my tongue as it darted in and back out. An experienced woman; the waitress's lips parted, and her pupils dilated. I had her.

"A beer." I rattled off a local brewery I'd seen they had on tap.

She was a full step away before Riley cleared her throat. "A soda, thanks."

I continued with the toothpick, leaning forward on my elbows on the table. I watched her track the slow push and pull of my tongue, keeping the toothpick in constant motion.

There were things I hadn't shown Riley, sexual experiences she'd yet to discover. But instinctively, her body knew. Her nostrils flared and color spread from her cheeks to her throat, and down to the dip of her cleavage. It was sexy, but whether she was mad or turned on, I couldn't tell. Hell, it might have been both.

Not that it mattered to me. I'd take her both ways.

She snapped her gaze away as the same blush darkened her cheeks. I couldn't help but chuckle and relax in the broken vinyl booth.

The eager waitress was back before Riley could fully compose herself. She placed Riley's drink before mine, and I made sure to brush my knuckles across her fingers as she handed me the beer glass.

After that she was purring baby this and sugar that, her panties probably already wet. As she took my order, she even rubbed the leather on my shoulder, dragging her fingers down and across my vice president patch.

Riley's seething glare could have peeled the fake lashes right off her eyes. With another flick of the toothpick, I nodded toward the angry, sexy as fuck woman across from me. In truth, the waitress didn't have a shot in hell.

Never would, because I'd had Riley.

"And for you?"

"A burger with cheese." Riley ground each syllable out with such hateful deliberation, I laughed.

When the waitress disappeared, I raised an eyebrow, still grinning. "Jealousy suits you."

"You're an asshole for leading her on like that." She huffed. Maybe not as jealous as I thought.

"Flirting doesn't make me a jerk unless the other person isn't feeling it. She is *one hundred percent* reciprocating."

"But you have no intention of sleeping with her, of seeing it through. You're just proving a point to me and your ego. So, who is the jealous one?" The angry mask faltered, just enough I could see the pain hiding there. "This is degrading."

I'd hurt her, not my intention. I'd only wanted to piss her off. "I'm not trying to fuck her, darlin.'"

"Then "—She made a small circle with her straw before dropping it in the soda. —"Why are you acting like this?"

"You ask too many damn questions." The rumble of straight piped exhaust and the bang of old, metal truck doors seeped through the walls as the jukebox switched songs.

We had a good twenty or more minutes before someone arrived to pick up Riley. Staying in a public place and flirting with the waitress kept us visible and Riley, for the most part, safe. Or so I hoped.

Twenty-Three

CAM

When the waitress dropped off the food, I put some juice behind my charm to prove a point. The waitress more than wanted it. And if Riley got pissed, decided being my ole lady was too much—that might be a good thing.

But fuck if hurting her didn't tear me apart.

Every word I said was hollow, but I made sure the waitress was eating it up, even brushed my knuckles across her breasts when I straightened her name tag. She didn't jump back or smack my hand away, instead leaned so close I could smell the tictac she'd popped before walking over.

"Now you're just being mean," Riley blurted when the waitress sauntered away, her eyes bright with unshed tears.

I needed to show her who I was, how life would be for her with me. Not because she'd done anything wrong, but because we were being followed, because my life was already putting her in danger.

Santos Garza had given her his number. I'd brought her there, I'd put her in his sites. Yeah, I hadn't expected the man himself, but I should have. She was right, part of the problem was my ego. As that had been what made me think I could keep her safe.

Archer had kept her safe, by keeping her away from here. Maybe I needed to do the same.

I'd do anything to keep her safe. She'd hate me for it, but wasn't this how it was always supposed to happen?

"Women like that, darlin, they ain't looking for a Prince Charming. Fifteen minutes with me would be the best day of her life. Women are easy."

Her confusion, the hurt feelings, were gone now. I'd hit my mark. "Is that the way you think about me?" There was a tremble to her bottom lip that punched me in the gut.

"You're nothing like that." Not even comparable.

"You screwed me, that the difference?"

I leaned over the table and for the first time in this whole fucked up charade, was brutally honest. "Because I *wanted* to fuck you, because I *want* to fuck you with every breath I take. Not because I'm doing either of us any favors."

The door swung open, letting in a momentary flash of sunlight as three white guys entered the bar. Two were scrawny skinheads. One was using, judging by the way he picked at the sores on his arms and twitched.

They all looked right at me. The one with the mullet jerked his eyes away fast and climbed onto a high-backed stool. I'd seen him when he'd driven past us. My hackles went up. Riley pushed at her burger, looked at it like there were worms crawling under the bun, and left it laying in the basket.

Plan B, Riley was staying with me.

I pulled out my phone to text Merc again. Not the group text, but Merc. My hesitation to alert everyone was the sort of thing that tore clubs apart. Archer had taught me that. But his blind trust had probably gotten him killed.

He taught me shit like that, too.

When the waitress came back, she slid a small piece of paper under my fingers. The red of Riley's cheeks darkened almost purple. She might not think she was jealous, but she was. Likely she thought this was my payback for Garza. And maybe it was.

The hairs on my arms prickled, my intuition telling me something bad was about to happen. My leg shook restlessly under the table—my body preparing for trouble.

When I fucked Riley, I let my guard down. Let myself forget who I was.

I wasn't leading the waitress on; I'd been leading Riley on. I hated myself for it. Deep down, knew I'd burn for it.

"What's going on?"

She was too perceptive. I glanced up from Merc's response.

If shit pops off, head to the clubhouse. Meet you there.

"Nothing."

"I'm seriously going to need you to respect me enough to stop lying to my face."

Why did she have to be so fucking cute with her righteous indignation? Her irritation was easier to deal with than the other emotions. I glanced over and caught Mullet watching us through the mirror behind the bar.

"There's so much shit happening right now, I don't know where to begin." A deflection, but fuck if it wasn't the truth.

"I'm good enough to screw but not good enough to talk to. Good to know." She pushed the basket back, stood with a grumbling mumble, and went to the bar.

The weathered bartender with the day's growth of white beard was more accommodating to her than the waitress had been. The rednecks following us were as well.

If I called her back, they'd know I was on to them. And that would cost me the element of surprise. Which I'd need to keep our asses intact.

I ate, but tasted nothing, and watched as Mullet chatted her up. The other two kept their distance for a while, focusing their attention on me. This guy was running the show. He was the one I'd take out first. Something else Archer had taught me, in a fight never stop moving, and cut the head off the snake.

With a crack of my neck, I drug a fry through ketchup and tossed it in my mouth. The waitress came back, and all but sat right in my basket of food when she propped a hip on the table.

Accustomed to women, to the shared way women like her put the moves on a guy, I only half listened. She tugged at the patches on my vest, working her way toward the t-shirt and my chest.

My attention was with Riley, especially when one of the skinheads flanked her. I took a few more bites of the burger as she caught my gaze in the mirror. Her discomfort was obvious, but she was too fucking stubborn to come back to me.

"A man like you needs a real woman." The waitress' laugh was low and sultry, her shorts inched up so high now they disappeared into her groin.

"Think so?"

"That little girl can't give you what you need."

Wrong again, lady.

I didn't hear anything else she said, as a familiar look furrowed Mullet's brow. He'd said the wrong something—and Riley was Archer's daughter. Her bristle was visible from across the room.

That was my cue. I took a fifty from my wallet and tossed it on the table.

"Hey, are you even listening, sugar?"

"Nope." I was on my feet, striding across the mostly empty seating area, before she had a chance to shout at me.

"Listen here, you mouthy bitch." Mullet grabbed Riley's arm and something flared white hot and deadly dangerous inside my chest.

Everything happened in a matter of seconds. There was a crackle and the snap of bone when I grabbed his hand and jerked it back, twisting his wrist and breaking a couple fingers in the process. His face contorted with pain.

Another thing Archer taught me: the elbow is the hardest point on the body and I needed my hands to ride. I smashed my left elbow into his face and threw him on the ground before the first skinhead scrambled toward me.

Riley smashed a glass right into his nose, blood and glass flying. He screamed like a bitch, grabbing at his face with both hands.

I don't think I'd ever been so proud in my life.

I punched the other skinhead before he could jump from his seat, and he folded over the side of it like a paper plate. Riley smacked against my chest, already running. Her gaze met mine as I moved, and there was an open realization in her eyes. She was far from stupid. Maybe she was more cut out for this life than I gave her credit for.

The anger that tingled through me, icy hot, was no doubt showing on my face. I damn sure wasn't trying to hide it. "Go!"

More were coming. Mullet was already on his phone. I hit the door and held it open for her, jumping on the bike and tossing her my phone.

"Text Merc that we're coming in hot!" I fired up the Harley.

As soon as her arms wrapped around my waist, I kicked up the stand and pitched the bike sideways, spitting gravel all over their big green truck.

I was in third gear, blasting down the highway before any of them made it from the parking lot.

A shrill, warm sound sang over the roar of the exhaust. I glanced over my shoulder to see Riley laughing with her face tilted toward the sun and her hair blowing behind her.

Something else licked against my rib cage, pushing away the anger and coating it with a warmth and comfort I'd never imagined possible.

I was a goner.

Twenty-Four

RILEY

The roar of the Harley was an angry reverberation that shot right through my chest and stole my breath. I wasn't scared, not as I should be. I trusted Cam's ability, but more...I knew that he'd keep me safe. Even if he didn't realize it.

I wasn't thinking about whatever had just happened. The washed-up server with more cheap makeup than good sense was a distant memory. I understood what he was doing now. I wasn't happy about it, but I got it.

He'd been trying to scare me off. Too bad, it wasn't going to work.

This blind trust was new, but it had been there since that moment in the bedroom when he'd taken Archer's pistol from me. Cam was different from anyone I'd ever met. Nothing was ever done without careful deliberation, without a reason.

He wasn't forgiven, but I shoved his phone in my pocket and clung tightly to his middle as we flew down the road. We were going so fast, the wind cut beneath my shades and pricked painfully at my skin.

I ducked my head against Cam's shoulder. There'd been no time for a helmet, it had bounced along the parking lot.

When I noticed him glancing in the mirror, I hazarded a look over my shoulder. In the distance, a big green truck was accelerating toward us. Cam took that moment to slide into the oncoming lane and pass two cars before swerving back into the right.

We are being chased.

Fear creeped in then. Our argument in the bar, the fight with the creepy guys, it was all sliding together. Cam had wanted me to find another ride home because he saw this coming. He'd been preparing for it—and instead of telling me the truth, he'd tried to manipulate me.

Stupid, stupid boy.

The moment we hit the county line, Cam shot up the exit ramp and blew past the stop sign. Two trucks now, getting closer as he wove in between traffic with deft movements. Leg out, he made a sharp turn onto a lane of broken pavement that slid between two rows of houses and then across an abandoned school parking lot.

He barely glanced to see if traffic was coming. I trembled a little but swallowed down the dread. If he lost control, even for a second, at these speeds—we were dead. If they caught us, who knew what might happen. I glanced down to the pistol in the holster at his back.

I'd never fired one, but I might need to learn.

This time when we roared through downtown, people looked out of sheer shock at the speed. I didn't even have time to register faces or signage. The buildings passed in such a blur that I'm surprised we didn't peel the bricks off and leave them in crumbling piles behind us.

When he turned, houses and bystanders grew farther and farther between. On either side of us, yards turned into desert that stretched out for as far as anyone could see. The road was winding, but I'd ridden it with Cam. He could take those curves much faster with little effort. He continued to glance in the rearview mirror now, as if ensuring they were close.

It wasn't until I saw familiar formations in the distance I recognized where he was heading. The back side of the MC's property was here. You had to drive right by it to get back to the highway and there weren't any other roads.

He was leading them into a trap.

My heart raced with excitement and my fear vanished in a burst of adrenaline. This was exhilarating, sexy. I'd learned enough to know that whatever was happening, the club wasn't going to let it stand.

There's something seriously wrong with you.

Cam accelerated hard out of the last turn and around a rocky hillside covered with short, squat trees. I could hear the roar then, louder than the pop and rumble of Cam's bike alone. The sound was more ebbing and throbbing until it was a symphony of angry steel.

As the clubhouse itself came into sight, so did the bikes. Twenty, maybe thirty of them, lining both sides of the pavement. A new, full-size truck sat sideways in the road, blocking traffic. Cam accelerated hard then, flying right toward the row of men in leather vests that stepped into the road, weapons drawn.

Never in my life would I have imagined rocketing toward gun barrels would be this thrilling.

At the last possible second, Cam braked, pitched the bike sideways, and slid to a stop. I held to him so tightly, I almost shot off the back as he slammed the kickstand to the ground and jumped off.

I stumbled as a gentle hand took my elbow and pulled me backwards. I glanced up to see Merc, a long rifle in his hand, pulling me toward the side of the road, shoving me behind him.

The two large trucks were slowing, another row of bikes following them in. Cam had pulled the pistol from the small of his back, held it up and pointed it directly at the driver of the green truck.

He was the one who had grabbed me in the bar. Cam marched to him, his face hard in profile, eyes narrowed. He moved with furious intent, every step like a punch to the frantic beat of my heart.

The truck stopped, and the driver slowly lifted both hands in the air as he looked past Cam to me. The smirk that spread across his face left me cold inside.

Beside me, Merc aimed his rifle. His line of sight was across the hood of the truck and into the desert. He pulled the trigger, the rifle crack barely audible over the panicked ringing in my ears. In front of Cam, the side-view mirror on the truck exploded into pieces. The passenger's hands shot straight up into the air in a sign of peace.

Cam didn't flinch. He yanked the door open and jerked the driver out onto the pavement. His face was red, his lips moving as he pushed the gun barrel against the guy's forehead.

My panic arced, changing to something else entirely. I had been afraid they would hurt Cam. Now, no one shot forward to stop him. This time when Merc grabbed me, it was with one strong arm around my middle as he shouldered the rifle with the other.

I was screaming, but no one seemed to care.

Preacher marched up the center line, shoulders back as if he were the king of this realm. Cam, the mad prince. He nudged Cam over, kicked at the redneck's shin, and shouted to the others. All the other skin head looking tweakers in the trucks sat frozen. Smart move.

Cam didn't holster his weapon as Preacher pushed the guy toward the truck but took several methodical steps backward. It was the easy way he held the gun, finger resting on the trigger. He'd kill them, every one of them.

I saw him differently then. In a way that should scare me all the way back to California, but it didn't. Somehow, I wanted him more.

Around us, bikes pulled off, surrounding the two trucks as Preacher issued orders I couldn't make out over the rumble. Cam's grip on the gun released as the trucks reversed, carefully making their way through a parted sea of bikers.

Those bikes followed them, much more slowly than they'd entered.

"An escort out of town," Merc told me, releasing his hold on me before deftly unloading his rifle and dropping ammo into his pocket. "Too many bodies to bury at once and the incinerator ain't big enough"

His delivery was so dry, I couldn't be sure if he was joking. I got a sinking feeling that he wasn't.

Cam finally holstered his gun as the trucks disappeared around the bend. Only a few of the men I knew to be officers followed. The rest hovered around Cam as he approached me.

And it was like no one else existed. Just him and I in the middle of the street, watching each other. Was he afraid I'd run? That I'd finally seen some part of him that should make me want to?

I didn't. I wouldn't. I couldn't.

We both moved at the same time, walking toward each other. He grabbed my hand, spinning back toward his bike. I climbed on as he drove the short distance to the clubhouse and parked with far more tact this time.

It wasn't until I watched him climb off that I realized his fingers trembled. I had a hard time believing anything could scare Cam Savage. He threaded those fingers through mine and pulled me close to his side. Merc and several others stopped him. This time it was Cam who barked orders.

"Table after the others get back. Get rid of everyone not patched in."

I figured that meant I was to leave, but he pulled me into the clubhouse behind him.

Krystal ran up, giddy with excitement. Admittedly, watching that smile slide from her face was one of the better moments in my life. No matter how small that made me.

"Fuck off, Krystal." He shoved her to the side with his free hand and stalked toward the stairs.

I only had a second to sneak a glance at her. She wasn't happy. I didn't care.

It wasn't until he shut the door behind us, I realized what he wanted.

What I needed.

Twenty-Five

RILEY

Riley

Cam's chest heaved, his blue eyes wide and wild, as he shoved his still shaky hand through his hair. Afraid to touch him, in case he exploded into a mess of adrenaline and chaos. I stood several feet away and watched him.

I didn't dare take my eyes from his.

He grabbed my face and kissed me hard. His lips and tongue as hot and urgent as the hell bent for leather ride we'd just been on. The hand that slid down my back and gripped my ass was just as dangerous.

He broke the kiss on a raspy moan and licked his lips. "I need you before I do something really stupid."

I shouldn't have been that turned on, but I was already wet for him. My body openly defying and betraying the anger that hummed somewhere beneath the desire. My physical need buried it, which was why I pressed my lips to his throat as I rubbed myself against him.

He shrugged out of his vest, slipped the holster and pistol from his side, and placed them on the ratty dresser by the door. The gun in his back followed, then leather and boots hit the ground with thuds as he walked me backward.

Cam kissed me the entire time. My lips, his tongue flicking against mine, my jaw, my neck, and lower across my cleavage as he pushed me onto the bed.

Hovering above me, a shock of blond hair falling into his face, he stopped. "I can't be easy, here, darlin." His entire body trembled now. When he pulled his shirt over his head and tossed it, the muscles across his chest quivered.

I reached out and brushed my fingertip across his chest before he caught my hand. "I mean it."

He was giving me an out, afraid that my lack of experience would make this a scary thing. It wouldn't. I trusted him. If he needed it rough, then I wanted it that way. Excitement lit, white hot and biting inside me when he shed the last of his clothes.

"Was everything you said at the bar bullshit?" But I had to know. "Is it just that you want to fuck me or is it something more?"

"So much fucking more." He came back to me, panting, nipping at my lip. "How could I want anyone else when I have you? I can't stop thinking about you, I can't picture anything else but you. Riley—it's you."

He cupped my groin, pushed his palm against the part of me that was already hot for him. My hips bucked. I should be shy, I wasn't. Maybe it was the adrenaline, or Cam himself, but every part of me was desperate for his hands, his mouth...for the cock that pressed against my thighs as he tugged at my waistband.

"Take it all off." It was me he barked orders at now, nipping through my shirt and down my stomach.

I did as commanded, pushing the shorts he'd unbuttoned down my hips.

"Leave the boots." He was already jerking my shirt up and over my head as I shifted. I couldn't be sure how I managed to wriggle free of my bra, but Cam's eyes caught mine when he clutched the crotch of my panties and gave them a tug.

His knuckles brushed my slit, and he watched me. "You want it bad, don't you?"

"Yes." I bucked again, and he jerked them all the way off.

Cam grabbed a condom from the tiny bedside table, ripped into the package with his teeth, and pushed it on in one quick, practiced motion. Then he tossed my boot clad legs over each of his arms and pressed into me.

Everything happened so fast. One second, I was trembling with anticipation and the next my legs were spread wide and my knees were pushed against my chest. I was full of him as he groaned low and long, his expression just as fierce as it had been when he'd pulled his gun.

My heated skin prickled, my breath caught, and when he moved, pleasure arced through me in electric bursts. Savage. His lovemaking then lived up to his name. Each thrust harder, faster, than the first, until all I could hear was our skin slapping and the bed creaking.

I gripped the multicolored crocheted blanket beneath me. My fingers slipped between the oversized holes and wrapped around as he arched, folding my body in what should be an impossible position.

This way, my knees over his elbows spread me so wide that it felt as if he might split me open. The friction built too fast, like my heart and my mind were racing to catch up with what he was doing to me.

Just like everything else.

I whimpered, moaned, and twitched as my orgasm raced closed.

"I want to hear it." He gasped. "I want them all to hear it, baby."

He thundered into me when I came. Not shy, no, not now and maybe never again. I came screaming. "Cam, Cam, Cam!" Over and over as pleasure rocketed with my orgasm, coating him, me, leaving me panting and my skin wet.

Several thrusts later, Cam tossed his head back and moaned long and loud before dropping my legs and collapsing heavily on top of me.

"Holy fuck." Was all he said between panted breaths.

And that summed it up perfectly.

***

Cam rolled off me and pulled me close, tucking me against his side. The music no longer beat from downstairs, so the only sound was our ragged breathing and the thump of Cam's heart against my face as I snuggled into his heaving chest. I got lost in the rhythm of it until my heart matched his. So much of my life was gone, dead, or taken away. But Cam was here, real, and alive.

When the air-conditioning kicked on and I shivered as the cool air met my slick, hot skin, he pulled the brown and orange blanket over us.

The rush of the chase, of the sex, faded and his pulse slowed. I was left floating on this buzz of misplaced emotion. I was strangely happy. Everything I'd been taught, society, and my life said I shouldn't be.

"Is it always like this?" I asked. My voice hoarse and my throat slightly sore from the chase, the aftermath, and then the sex.

"Sex?" He was sleepily confused, stretched out beneath me like a sated cat.

"All of it. Today, the sex, this part..." The last being the most important. I didn't realize how much it was until I lay there with Cam holding me. I needed this intimacy that filled an empty place inside me I hadn't realized existed.

"Yes—no." His chest shifted on a deep exhale. "I'm sorry about all that shit today. But I can't say it's not normal." His voice was all rough and sexy. "It used to not be, but—" Then he chuckled. "The sex gets better each time I'm inside you. Who knew you were so hot in bed?"

I sat up and smacked him square on the stomach. He oofed a laugh. "I'm serious. You're the best I've ever had."

When I shot him a yeah right look, he sighed, thought about it, then climbed from the bed and padded to the bathroom. I watched him. His ass was firm and tight. I'd never thought a guy's ass could be so hot and yet his was.

The water turned on and he came back, cleaned up, and crawled on the bed with me. "Every damn thing about you is fucking perfect. And I'm the only man on the planet to have that." He kissed me, softly at first, then with more heat. "And that's unbelievably sexy. Makes me want you again and again, as many times a day as you'll let me."

The passion from his words turned me inside out, and the way his lips trailed down my jaw and my neck was so arousing I almost gasped. Even after all of this, Cam's kiss and touch were so thrilling it almost scared me.

His cock was hard against my stomach as he shifted and lay me back on the bed, crawling over me, sucking a nipple into his mouth, then switching to the other while his hands stroked everywhere lighting little fires up my sides.

"Again? Right now?" I asked with an excited squeak.

"Mhmm." His voice vibrated around my nipple.

The loud, throbbing reverberation of an army of Harley Davidson's returning earned a groan from him as he rolled away. "Rain check, I've got some shit to handle."

That was an understatement. The past few hours had been like something out of an action-packed movie. All adrenaline, sensation, and emotion. I watched him as he moved around the room, getting dressed in the same efficient motions as he did everything. He was perfectly at home here, in what I could only describe as a teenage boy's crash pad. Complete with posters of bikini-clad models draped all over shiny black and chrome motorcycles.

"You can hang out here until I get back or walk downstairs and make yourself a drink. If anyone is still here, it'll be Dylan."

I moved on the bed and struggled a bit to pull my panties and shorts back over the boots. "I can walk down with you." The idea of staying up there alone made me uneasy. I didn't want to be far from Cam, not here.

He waited at the door and lit a cigarette, shoving his lighter in his pocket before taking my hand in his free one and walking down the stairs with me. Krystal and the other groupies were long gone. A small handful of bikers were rolling in, somber. Every so often, one would break off from a group and head to the hallway with those two heavy oak doors.

Merc waited at the base of the stairs, lounging against the rail, unbothered and disinterested, like nothing important had just happened. He nodded once to me. "Dylan's in the kitchen, getting food together."

What he wasn't saying was *if you don't want to stay out here with all of them.* Men in leather vests lingered in the main room, one behind the bar passing out beers. They all watched me until Cam gave a hard glare.

He kissed the top of my head and used his hand on the back of my neck to steer me in that direction. "Get something to eat. This won't take long."

Walking away wasn't easy, but like Dylan had said, there were things we weren't meant to know. And while I didn't like it, I was starting to understand. Today had been eye opening in many ways.

I ignored the leering stares and pushed through the steel industrial style door and into the commercial sized kitchen. It smelled of some sort of roast and vegetables, savory, and onions. Dylan was leaned over a large pan, pulling the aluminum foil back and poking inside with a large fork.

She looked so calm and at ease, so normal that I felt bad about our argument. "Hey."

She glanced up and hesitated before responding with a cautious, "You okay?"

"Yeah." It wasn't a lie. "I feel like I should be more traumatized, but I'm not."

"Cam's not going to let anything happen to you." She hefted out another pan and then pulled down two plates. Her blind trust in him gave me the warm fuzzies.

"I'm sorry, Dylan. About last night and everything."

She waved it off. "Don't be. Seriously. I think we understand each other." She caught my gaze and held it in such a way I knew she meant what she said.

"Yeah, we do." I waited a minute, peaked under the tinfoil at the meat settled in thick gravy. "But you were right, you are a bitch."

Dylan's laugh was as rich as the gravy.

And this is what it felt like to make my first true friend. Someone other than Cam, who understood me.

Twenty-Six

CAM

Leaving Riley got harder and harder each time I did it. I could kid myself that I watched her walk away to make sure she was safe, not the overwhelming urge to look at her. The way the boots accentuated her long legs all the way to that tight ass drove me out of my mind. I'd just had her, and somehow my cock twitched to life again.

I took a deep breath and forced those thoughts away. She glanced over her shoulder at me, caught my gaze, and flashed me a shy, knowing smile.

Mine.

And she was the sexiest goddamned thing I'd ever seen. Two parts of me warred against each other. One wanting her gone, knowing she'd be trouble for us both if she stayed and the other that would do anything to keep her.

Preacher, the Club, losing Archer...none of it mattered when I was with her, when I was lost inside her. I'd never imagined it possible for me to be so consumed.

I'd seen guys be so twisted from drugs or alcohol that they couldn't focus, lost control of their lives, and ended up in jail or worse—losing their patches. But none of that had ever been a problem for me. Hell, the only thing in life I could get addicted to was Riley Bowman.

A hand smacked me on the shoulder with the familiar thump of a long-standing friendship. Puck had patched in a few years after Merc and I, but had always hung around the two of us. To the point Archer had affectionately called us knuckleheads. I rubbed the patch opposite my VP patch, the one that Archer had made for the three of us.

Felt like someone was punching me there. I reached into my pocket and twisted the old man's bike key around. Keeping him close.

"You good, brother?" Puck's eyes creased around the corners as he studied me.

"Yeah." I was whole, so was Riley. And now that the adrenaline had faded and I could assess myself, I was pissed. "Still want to hit something." Or someone.

"Maybe you'll get a chance." He sneered with a short laugh and tied his hair back.

"He one of them?" Puck's ex-ole lady had messed around with one of the peckerwoods.

"Yeah, you pulled a damn gun on his ass." He chuckled. "I was half hoping you'd shoot the bastard."

I almost had. The fierce protective instinct wrapped me up so tight I paused in the doorway to the chapel. I glanced across the room, more dark paneled meeting space than actual place of worship. Though the reverence we showed this room was very similar.

Preacher sat in Archer's seat. It made me angry. I shook that off and took my place directly to his left, AP sitting across from me. The other guys spread out around us. Not assigned seating, but everyone knew where to go.

When the thick door thudded shut and the lock clicked, I took the fat envelope from my vest, and plucked the individually wrapped stacks of cash from inside. The stack of bills was substantial and had weighed heavy in my cut. I racked the cash against the table, watching Preacher's fingers twitch to reach for it, and then passed the money to AP to count as he always did. He split the stack, counted out most of the cash, passing that portion to Merc, and then racked the remaining bills against the table before turning to stash them in the safe.

Why would Preacher want the cash? The treasurer counted it, kept it, and put it away. Always had. He only passed the Ukrainian's part to Merc.

When I looked up, Merc frowned just a little. He'd seen it too.

"All there?" Preacher's voice was strained, the corners of his eyes tight.

Maybe I was imagining shit because I wanted somewhere to focus the anger that burned in my chest, and made my entire body vibrate. I didn't know where it came from or what it meant, just that I didn't like how shit was shaking down. I'd reached my limit with it.

"Think I'd short the Club, Preach?"

The dull murmur of conversation around the table stopped so suddenly that I almost thought it had been swallowed up by the roar of blood in my ears. To his dad's right, Merc's head snapped up, and he shot me a look that was half warning, half question.

Both Preacher's bushy eyebrows flicked up in shock, but there was a callousness in his beady eyes. "Intentionally, no. But you've been distracted."

"*Distracted*?" I enunciated the word slowly, each syllable filled with more petulance than the first. "How's that?"

"Break in at Archer's, the girl showing up right under your nose, now this." He flipped his hand up. "Ain't like you, Cam."

I leaned back in my seat, flexing my fingers as I crossed my arms over my chest. The urge to sock him right in his smug mouth was so strong I half thought I might do it. "A bunch of peckerwoods chasing me through the desert is my fault?"

"You took the girl, put her in danger, and you rode alone to meet the Mexicans when you shouldn't have—"

I slapped my open palm on the table. "It's been your idea all along that we split up, make it look less like a money drop—"

"You made the call, Savage. *You*. Taking the girl was stupid, you were paying more attention to her than your surroundings and got made. If it wasn't for the pretty little piece of pussy you got strapped to your ass, you wouldn't have made that mistake!"

I was on my feet, Puck's big arm around my chest before I could blink. I didn't care what he accused me of, but talking like that about Riley...

"Watch your fucking mouth, Preach." My voice sounded feral, wrong, and not my own.

Preacher stood slowly, knuckles on the large table in front of him, his arms outstretched as he hovered like a gorilla. "This is *exactly* what I'm talking about.

"You took Archer's kid past county lines twice, alone, within weeks of his death. Ro told me about your visit when I stayed over there last night. Archer's kid has got you thinking crazy, pissing off rednecks in bars, and starting shit you can't handle."

"Cam." Merc's voice was all warning, and unease travelled across the rest of the table, bodies shifting restlessly in the brief silence. Preacher and I were top of the food chain, the buck stopped with us. For the rest of the guys, Mom and Dad were fighting, and they didn't know what to do.

I had to calm down before I did something stupid. The edges of my vision were clouding the way it did when...bad shit happened. When he couldn't get close to Riley, he'd went for Ro. And she hadn't told me.

With a hard shrug, I flung Puck's arm off me, straightened my cut and slid into the chair. Any point I wanted to make about my relationship with Riley, he was going to make about Ro. He'd been after her for years.

I pulled out a cigarette and lit it. "When's the damn benefit ride Dylan has planned?"

Preacher nodded, as if that was done. It wasn't. I sat in my seat, listening to club business. It wasn't business as usual, hadn't been since Archer died. Preacher could blame Riley all day long, but if I was all twisted up, it wasn't because of her. It was because Archer hadn't killed himself, and I knew it to the depth of my soul.

The Desert Kings weren't whole, wouldn't be, until we did something about that.

As they droned on with the meeting, I kept replaying that day in my head. Finding out Archer was dead had rocked me, reminded me of the person I'd been when Archer had saved me. I was so close to falling back to that and then I'd found Riley sneaking around in the house and everything changed.

I had purpose. Hell, this time Archer's daughter was the one saving me from myself.

"All right, let's talk about the peckerwoods." Preacher looked around the table, his gaze finally landing on me with a half-bored expression, like he already knew the answer. "What happened?"

"Noticed a truck following me, stopped to eat. When we left, they chased me." Simple. To the point. No bullshit. That was the biggest different between Preacher and Archer. Preach talked in circles, Archer didn't. And Archer had made me.

"Know why?" This from Puck beside me.

"Nope. They were on me almost as soon as I left the meet, like they knew we'd be there."

"Bullshit." Preacher spat, rolling his eyes. "These guys are tweakers. Meeting place changes every time. They probably just followed you out."

"They didn't." I levelled my gaze on his and left it there, challenging him to doubt me.

Jester piped up. "Cam's too smart. He'd have noticed them at the diner. And if he hadn't, the cartel damn sure would have. They had to pick him up after he left the drop."

Preacher had already argued with me at the table, made a scene. He wasn't about to press someone else. I added Jester to the list of guys who probably had my back. I hated that I was doing that, questioning the loyalty of my brothers.

"So now what?" Preacher moved on.

"Go down to the trailer park, fuck some shit up, send them a message." Jester again, but the jovial nature of his tone was a testament to how much he'd enjoy doing that.

"Let's do it. I can't stand those white-trash tweakers." From someone else down the table.

"Retaliate against something that could have been avoided?" Preacher spoke at me, like he was chiding a child—something Archer had never done, even when I was young and hotheaded. "Nah, the Kings are better than that."

This time it wasn't Merc who whispered, "Easy," but AP from across the table. That Preacher dug at me twice meant he was baiting me, trying to make me pop off. I didn't need AP to remind me of that. I saw it coming.

"How's that?" Merc asked him.

"It's not just that she's a hot piece of snatch," Preacher grumbled. "She's Archer's kid, and he had enemies."

"Especially the peckerwoods," Drop Top added. "His beef with them went way back. Preacher's right, you shouldn't have been riding out of town with her alone. Not so soon after..." He trailed off, not wanting to finish that sentence.

There was a huge part of me poised to argue, but he wasn't wrong.

Smug because someone had made his point for him, Preacher shook his head at me like a sad parent. "I told you not to bring her. We should have left her with one of the guys who could have showed her a real ride." He guffawed, and several of the others chuckled nervously with him.

I counted four who didn't. AP, Merc, Jester, and Puck. Every part of my body went rigid. Merc slid his seat back, a barely perceptible move, in case he had to stop me if I went for the older fucker? No. His cool eyes were dark.

Ride or die, he'd roll with me no matter how I handled this. And that stopped the words on my tongue and stilled the hands I'd fisted in my lap. If I went for Preacher, it would tear the Kings apart. But there was something I could do.

If I was drawing a line, I was going to shove it down Preacher's throat.

"Any man at this table, or in this club, goes near my ole lady, I promise you I will fuck up your entire world." I let my grin slide, mean and possessive. "I'll burn it to the ground."

Merc whooped a laugh so loud that the echoes of it resounded around me. Jester leaned across the table, grinning big and slapping me on the shoulder. "Damn it, man, she's a good one."

"Archer's rolling in his grave." AP snorted, but his eyes were bright.

Staking my claim shifted the room, made it lighter. I levelled my gaze on Preacher and held it there, a clear challenge.

"Sounds like she's getting all the rides she needs from Savage." Jester clutched at his stomach, this time laughing.

The mood of the room shifted. The newest Patch at the table, Paul, looked around dumbstruck. Only minutes before, we'd been halfway to war.

"I say we send a couple of the guys—I think even that Ghost kid has some contacts—and have them ask questions. If we don't like the answers, we set a meet with Wanda." AP threw out the only reasonable way to go.

The queen of the trailer park. Her sons might act like they ran that shit, but Wanda was the OG desert meth cook, and she ran the whole damn scene. Normally she wasn't a problem for us, but her boys had never chased one of us through town, either.

"And if we don't like that, then we fuck shit up." Jester, still grinning, looked to AP for approval, and he nodded.

Preacher's face was like granite, each line like a roadmap that told the story of being rode hard and put away wet. "I'll take the new kid and Ghost and check it out myself."

"Fight night," Drop Top Randy said. "Let's iron that out before Merc heads to the Black Cat. You know the Ukrainians get a hard on for this shit."

The rest of the meeting went by like usual, leaving me tossing everything around in my head. When things slowed down, when I could think, I wanted to think about Riley. Especially the defiant way she'd told me to fuck off at that bar, then stood up to the rednecks.

It wasn't until we were filing out of the room that it hit me. "Yo, Preacher."

The burly man's brow furrowed as he paused, half standing from the table. Around us, everyone hung back listening, waiting on a bomb to drop.

I tossed down a grenade. "Garza wants a meet, just you. Says its personal."

Gesturing to Merc, I ducked off down the hall ignoring Preacher's dumb-struck gaze. Whatever the cartel wanted, couldn't be good. And his reaction told me he didn't want the club to know.

Now they did.

"What was that?" Merc hissed in a whisper, looking over his shoulder.

I shrugged, because there was more, waited until no one else filed out and Preacher was behind those doors alone, pulling his shit together before facing everyone after that.

"Nobody that associates with the club was in that bar," I whispered under my breath. "I never said where we stopped."

Merc's brow furrowed. "Brother..."

"I know." Because that meant Preacher knew a good deal more about the peckerwoods than he let on.

"Think they knew you had that much cash?"

It was more than most people saw in a lifetime. I didn't need to count it like AP had to know that. "Yup."

There wasn't anyone else I trusted with my suspicions.

He brooded in a way that was innately my best friend, brow furrowed like he was about to say something really fucked up. "Think he might owe Garza?"

My silence told him exactly what I thought.

Merc changed the subject as we walked out of the hallway and into the main part of the clubhouse, passing other guys. "Riding to the Cat with me?"

Ride or die.

"Yeah..." I glanced to where Riley was walking out of the kitchen.

"Better get permission before we leave the valley." I snorted. I was still mad, but burying it was easier the second I saw her.

"From her or Preach? The Black Cat might not be her style."

Oh, I was betting it was more her style than even I imagined. Riley was full of surprises.

Twenty-Seven

RILEY

I must have looked toward the hallway one too many times.

"Chapel can last hours, if something big is going on," Kenna piped up from her seat at the small table with us. She expertly ran a polish brush across a perfectly manicured fingernail and held it up for inspection. "And I'd say being chased through town by a bunch of meth heads is a lot."

"There was a fight," I whispered.

"With the peckerwoods?" Dylan popped the top off of a bottle of beer and stashed the flat opener in her back pocket as she sat down. "Or with you and Cam?"

I flinched. "Both."

When they stared at me, I shrugged and gave them the cliff notes version of my argument with Cam.

"He's an asshole." When Kenna flashed her a surprised look, Dylan chuckled. "I can say that. You didn't deserve him being a prick, but he was doing the same thing I tried to do. Warn you off, show you what this life is really like."

I stiffened. "After what just happened, I'd say I've had a really good taste of it."

"And?" Finished with her nails now, Kenna stole my soda and took a sip. "You going to run?"

Leather clad bikers filed out of the hallway. I watched them, prickles of excitement threading through me as I looked for Cam. When I saw him, head low, talking to Merc, I was certain I wasn't scared. "Nope. Not even close."

Kenna whooped a cheer, and Dylan smiled approvingly. Whatever had happened between us was gone. It wasn't just Cam. I was making real friends here for the first time in my life.

I was almost to him, ready to feel his arm draped over my shoulder, to find out what came next before Preacher stepped into my path. The beefy, older man always made me uncomfortable. Today wasn't any different. But the way he looked at me was. Whatever fake generosity he'd shown me at the funeral, even at my father's house, was long gone.

"I heard you were going through Archer's things. Find anything interesting? He's got a lot of shit, I'm sure, especially if you didn't know him." He tried to sound friendly but failed.

All the little sirens inside me that the adrenaline rush of the day brought to the surface revved their engines. I thought of the guns I'd found with Cam, Dylan, and Merc. But said nothing. Sure, the Desert Kings were all about loyalty, but it seemed like Cam and Merc were an island all on their own with this.

I'd protect that.

"Not really. Mostly pictures, clothes."

He grunted like he didn't believe me. And something similar to fear coiled in my belly. Who knew, being scared made me mouthy and left more than a good bit of accusation in my tone. "Maybe whoever broke in found all the interesting things."

I should have looked away, like the frightened cat he wanted me to be, but I didn't.

He kept his composure even as anger flared his nostrils. "You should be hearing from the lawyer soon."

Next week, not that I was telling him that. My intuition was that Preacher was bad news. Cam hadn't come out and said it, but he didn't give me the warm fuzzies AP or the others did. I had a hard time believing this man was Archer's best friend.

"I guess so." Playing dumb, I looked past him to where Merc and Cam had stopped to talk with Dekes.

When I tried to walk away, the large, barrel-chested man wedged himself between me and the hallway. To get away, I'd have to turn back and run back to the girls or shout for Cam, which would cause more problems.

"The club will need to know what's in the will. And I'll need to come by. Archer had some things that belonged to me."

"I'm sure you can talk to Cam about all of that. I'm really not—"

"Cam isn't Archer's kid, darlin. That's you." His bullying tone made me feel sick, my bravado fading.

I glanced over his shoulder, willing Cam to look my way.

"And I'm sure there'll be money. That's why you're here, ain't it? Homeless, looking for a handout."

How did he know anything about me? I'd only told Cam, and if he told anyone, it wasn't Preacher. I grew cold and wrapped my arms around myself to keep my hands from trembling. He wasn't wrong, but he wasn't right either.

"That's not exactly what—"

"The Kings can buy the house from you and any other property he has."

Why did he care so much about buying me off?

"That won't be necessary, really. I'm thinking about staying around for a while."

He snorted and sneered. "Must have found enough to set you up for a while, huh? Feel taken care of now?"

Finally, Cam looked up at me, read the situation correctly, and stalked toward us in a way all too familiar. It was like the bar and the rednecks, round two. "Cam takes care of me just fine."

I pushed past Preacher as he blustered and threw myself down the hall.

I slowed as soon as I got to Cam, wrapped both arms around his middle, under the cut, and plastered myself to him like a horny groupie. He stopped, body hard and tense, expression... worse than it had been today after the chase.

This was dangerous, savage, and any other time would make me want him so bad my toes would curl.

But not now.

"Preacher!" he called, his voice hollow and hard.

I squeezed harder. "Not here, Cam. Please."

This was the cold slither of fear snaking around all my possible futures. Preacher scared me, not just physically. There was a meanness to him, one that could lash out and hurt Cam. The bar had shown me a glimpse of what he was capable of. But this was different.

My fear was that Preacher could take him away from me.

To keep Cam Savage, I'd do just about anything.

Part Two: Vicious Heart

Coming November 2024

More From Candi Scott Fashionista's Playbook

Also Available from Leslie Scott

The Arkadia Fast Series

The Finish Line

Hot Lap

Full Tilt Boogie

And

Two Hearts, One Stone

About the Author

Candi Scott is the nom de plume of award winning author Leslie Scott. She has been writing stories for as long as she can remember. From kissing books to biker demi-demons and swamp witches she lives vicariously through each and every character. When not writing she lives and writes amidst her own happily ever after with her not so charming prince where they flirt relentlessly like twelve-year-olds and embarrass her teenage son. There's also domestic zoo wrangling, homeschooling, and animal rescue organization volunteering.

Find out more at Candi's Website

Printed in Great Britain
by Amazon